Q & RAY

·CASE #3·
FOUL PLAY AT ELM TREE PARK

TRISHA SPEED SHASKAN

ILLUSTRATED BY STEPHEN SHASKAN

Graphic Universe™ · Minneapolis

For my brother, Jesse, for taking me out to
the ball game and being an all-time great.
Love you! —TSS

To Greg Hunter and Emily Harris, for believing
in this series and helping make it the best it
could be —SS

Graphic Universe™
A division of Lerner Publishing Group, Inc.
241 First Avenue North
Minneapolis, MN 55401 USA

For reading levels and more information, look up this title at www.lernerbooks.com.

Main body text set in CCDaveGibbonsLower 11.5/13.25.
Typeface provided by ComicCraft.

Library of Congress Cataloging-in-Publication Data

Names: Shaskan, Trisha Speed, 1973– author. | Shaskan, Stephen, illustrator.
Title: Foul play at Elm Tree Park / written by Trisha Speed Shaskan ; illustrated by Stephen Shaskan.
Description: Minneapolis : Graphic Universe, [2018] | Series: Q & Ray ; case #3 | Summary: Hedgehog Quillan Hedgson, a.k.a Q, and rat Ray Ratzberg are second-grade students and sleuths who use handwriting analysis and photographic evidence to solve the case of a stolen autographed baseball. | Description based on print version record and CIP data provided by publisher; resource not viewed.
Identifiers: LCCN 2017044293 (print) | LCCN 2017058393 (ebook) | ISBN 9781541523784 (eb pdf) | ISBN 9781512411492 (lb : alk. paper) | ISBN 9781541526440 (pb : alk. paper)
Subjects: LCSH: Graphic novels. | CYAC: Graphic novels. | Mystery and detective stories. | Stealing–Fiction. | Penmanship–Fiction. | Hedgehogs–Fiction. | Rats–Fiction.
Classification: LCC PZ7.7.S455 (ebook) | LCC PZ7.7.S455 Fo 2018 (print) | DDC 741.5/973–dc23

LC record available at https://lccn.loc.gov/2017044293

Manufactured in the United States of America
1-39658-21287-2/27/2018

WHO'S WHO

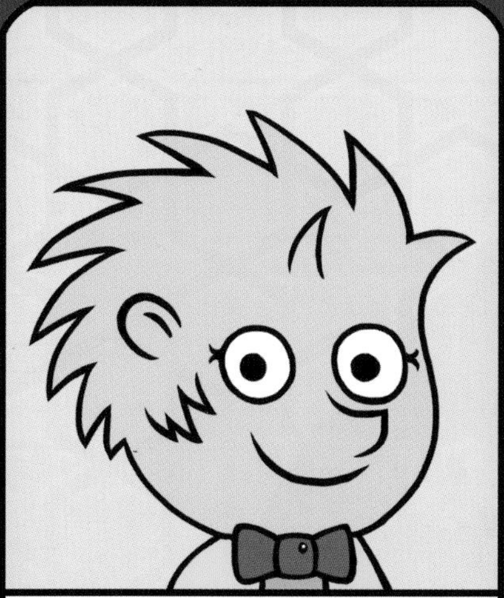

Quillan Lu Hedgeson
aka: Q

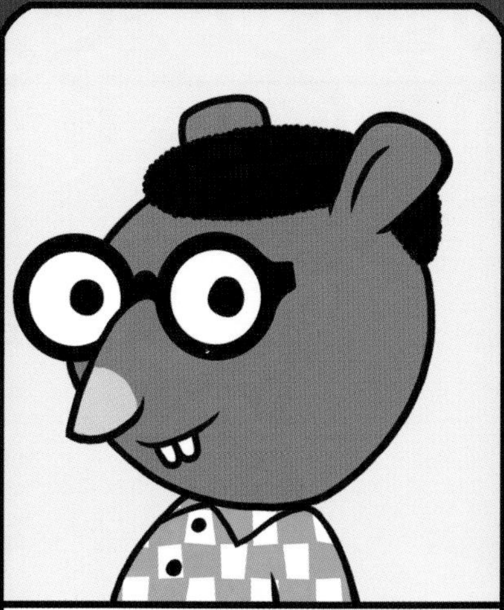

Ray Ratzberg

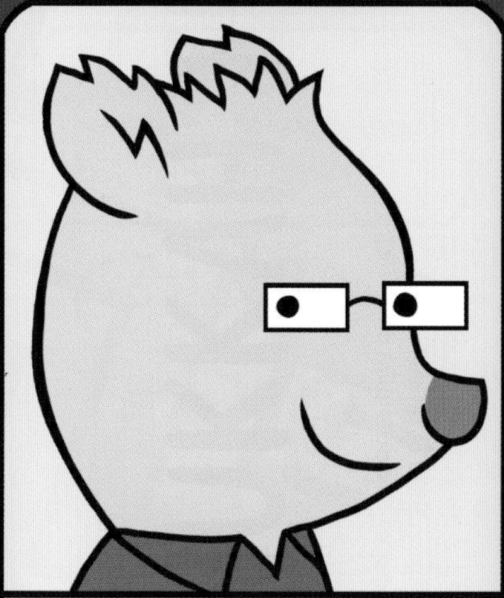

Mr. Shrew
Media Specialist

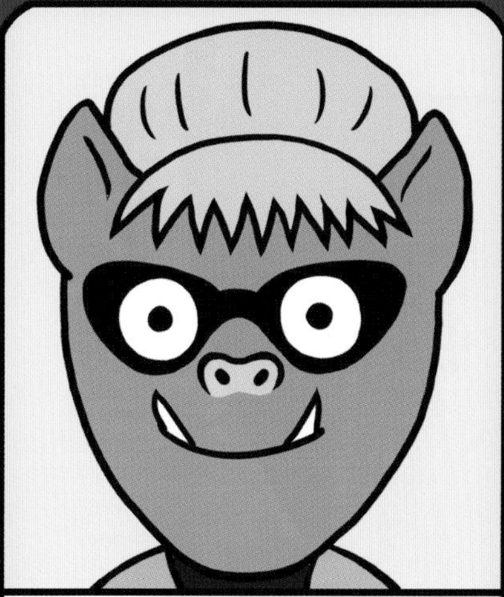

Ms. Boar
Classroom Teacher

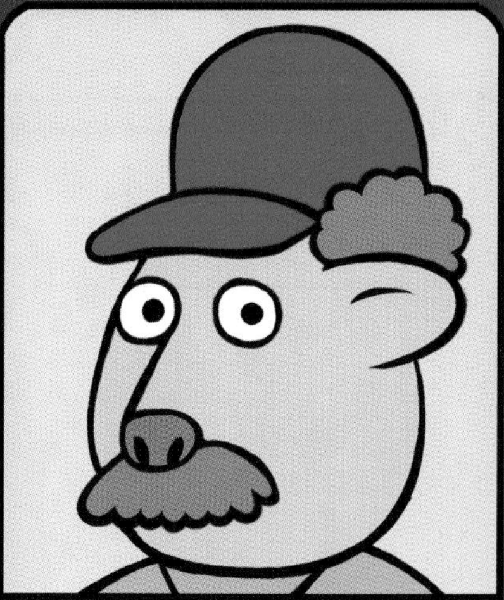

Mr. Teecher
Gym Teacher

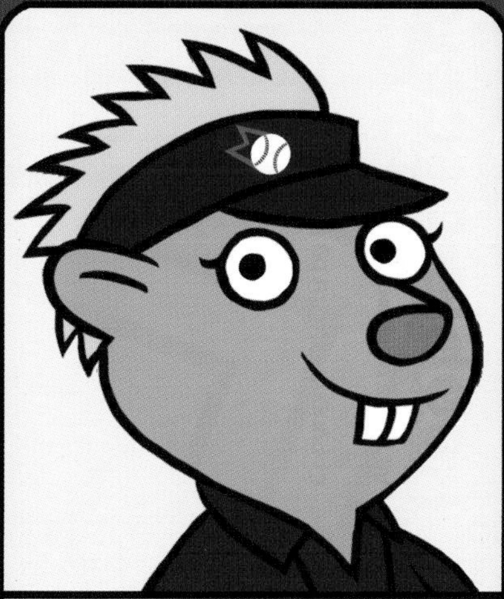

Gloria Gopher
Elm Tree Park Guide

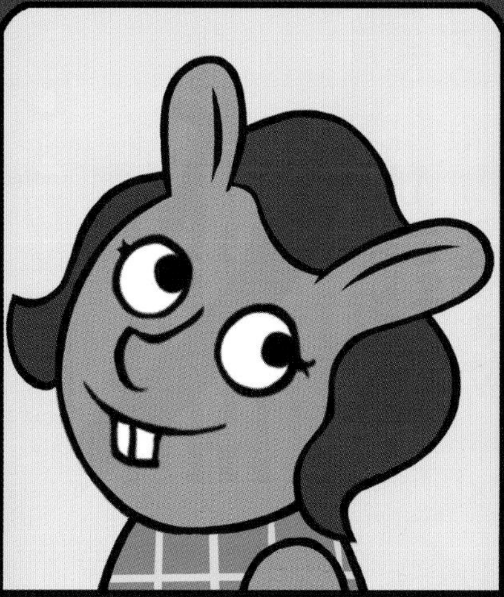

Satin

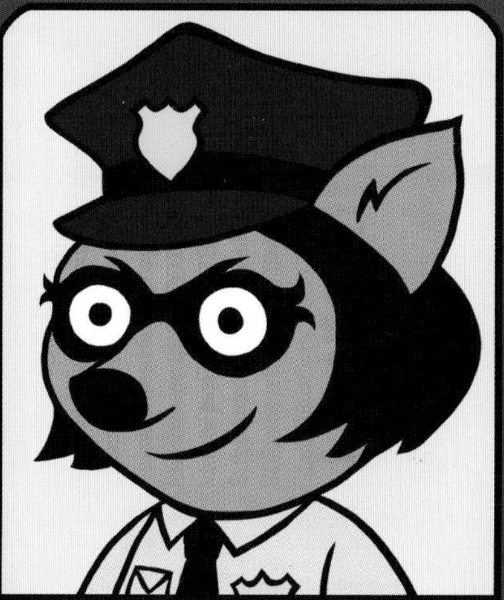

Officer Rocco

CHAPTER ONE
Baseball and Forgery

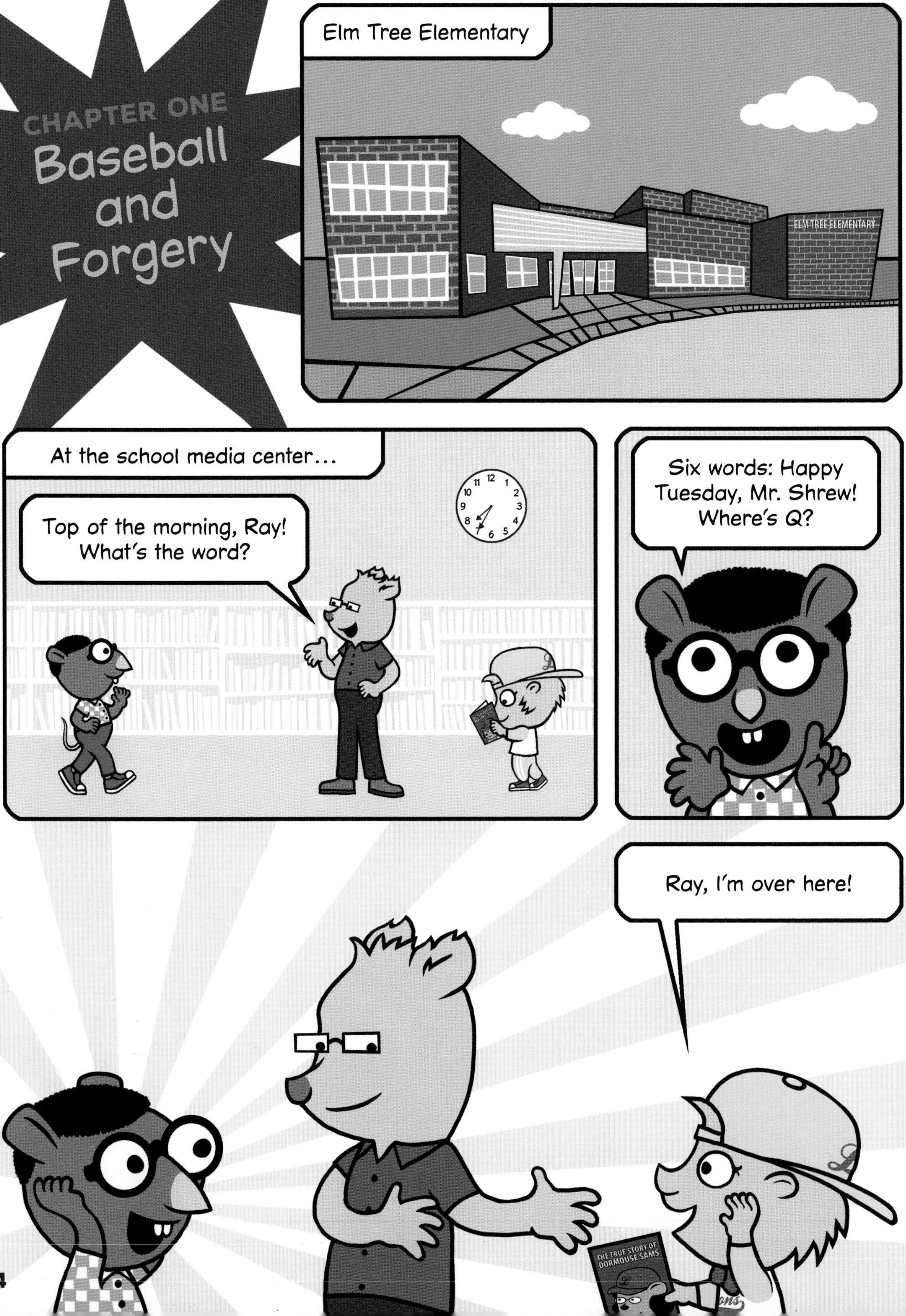

Elm Tree Elementary
ELM TREE ELEMENTARY
At the school media center...
Top of the morning, Ray! What's the word?
Six words: Happy Tuesday, Mr. Shrew! Where's Q?
Ray, I'm over here!
THE TRUE STORY OF DORMOUSE SAMS

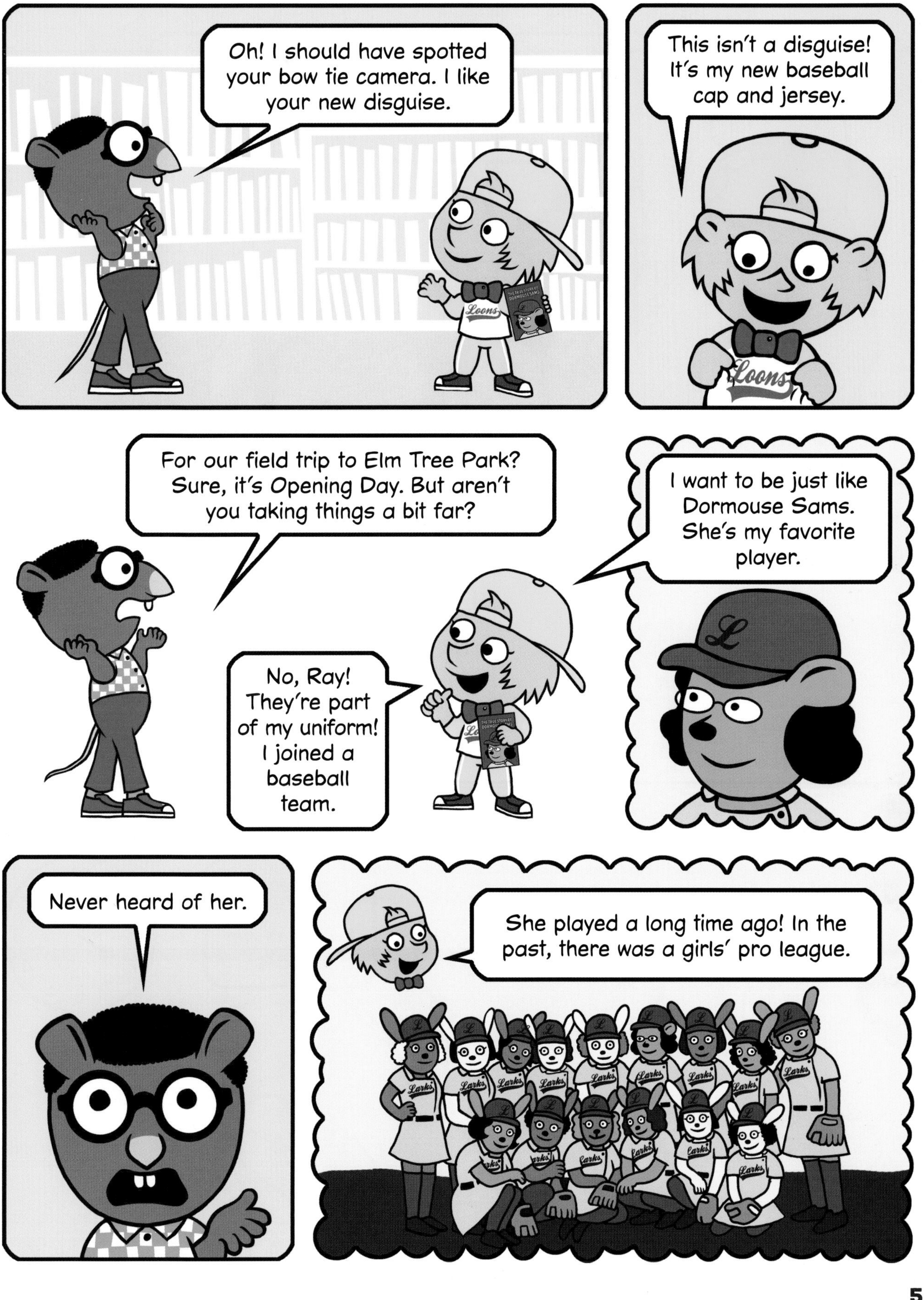
Oh! I should have spotted your bow tie camera. I like your new disguise.
This isn't a disguise! It's my new baseball cap and jersey.
For our field trip to Elm Tree Park? Sure, it's Opening Day. But aren't you taking things a bit far?
No, Ray! They're part of my uniform! I joined a baseball team.
I want to be just like Dormouse Sams. She's my favorite player.
Never heard of her.
She played a long time ago! In the past, there was a girls' pro league.
Loons
Larks

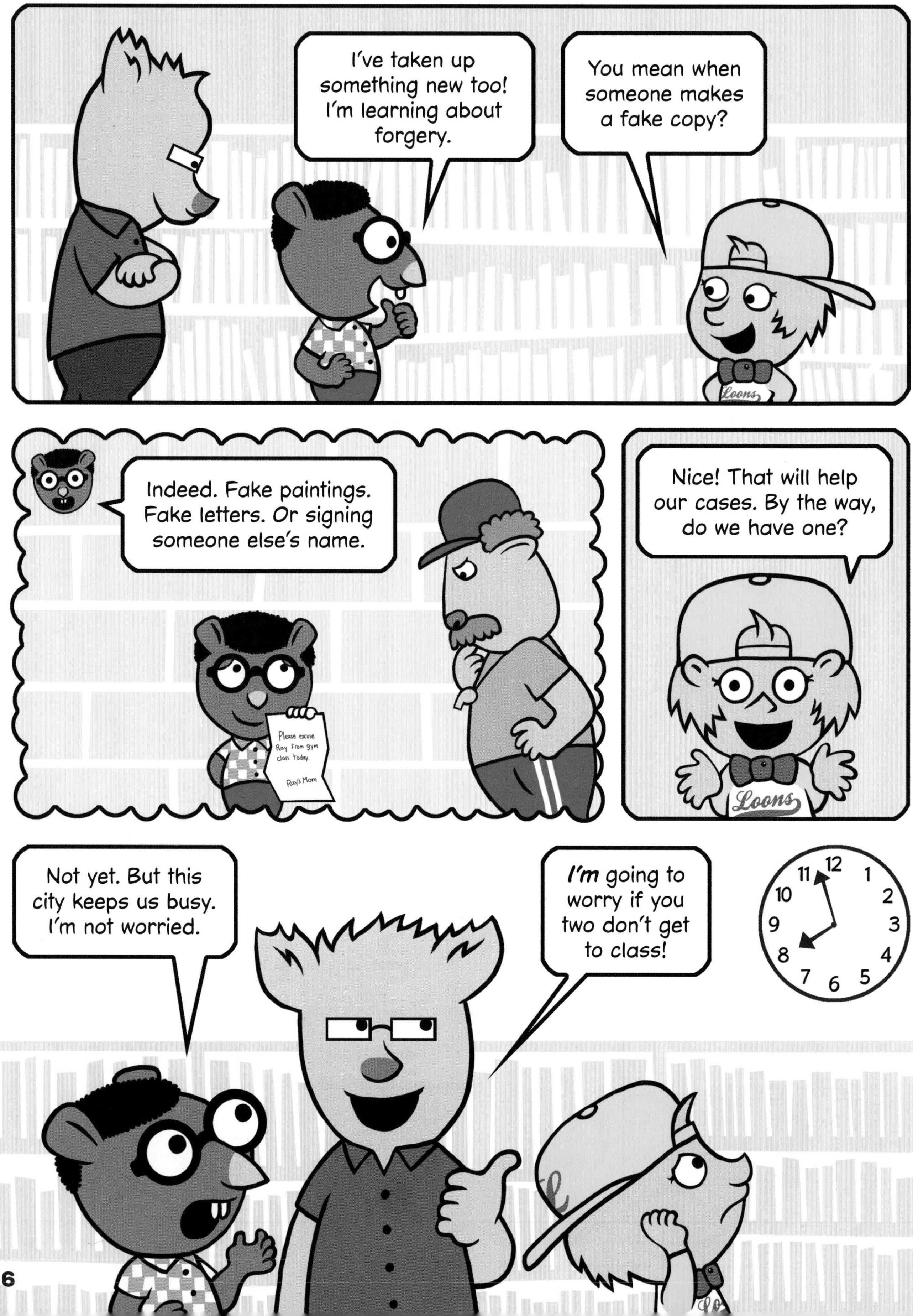
I've taken up something new too! I'm learning about forgery.
You mean when someone makes a fake copy?
Loons
Indeed. Fake paintings. Fake letters. Or signing someone else's name.
Please excuse Ray from gym class today. Ray's Mom
Nice! That will help our cases. By the way, do we have one?
Loons
Not yet. But this city keeps us busy. I'm not worried.
I'm going to worry if you two don't get to class!
12 1 2 3 4 5 6 7 8 9 10 11

CHAPTER TWO
What a Catch!

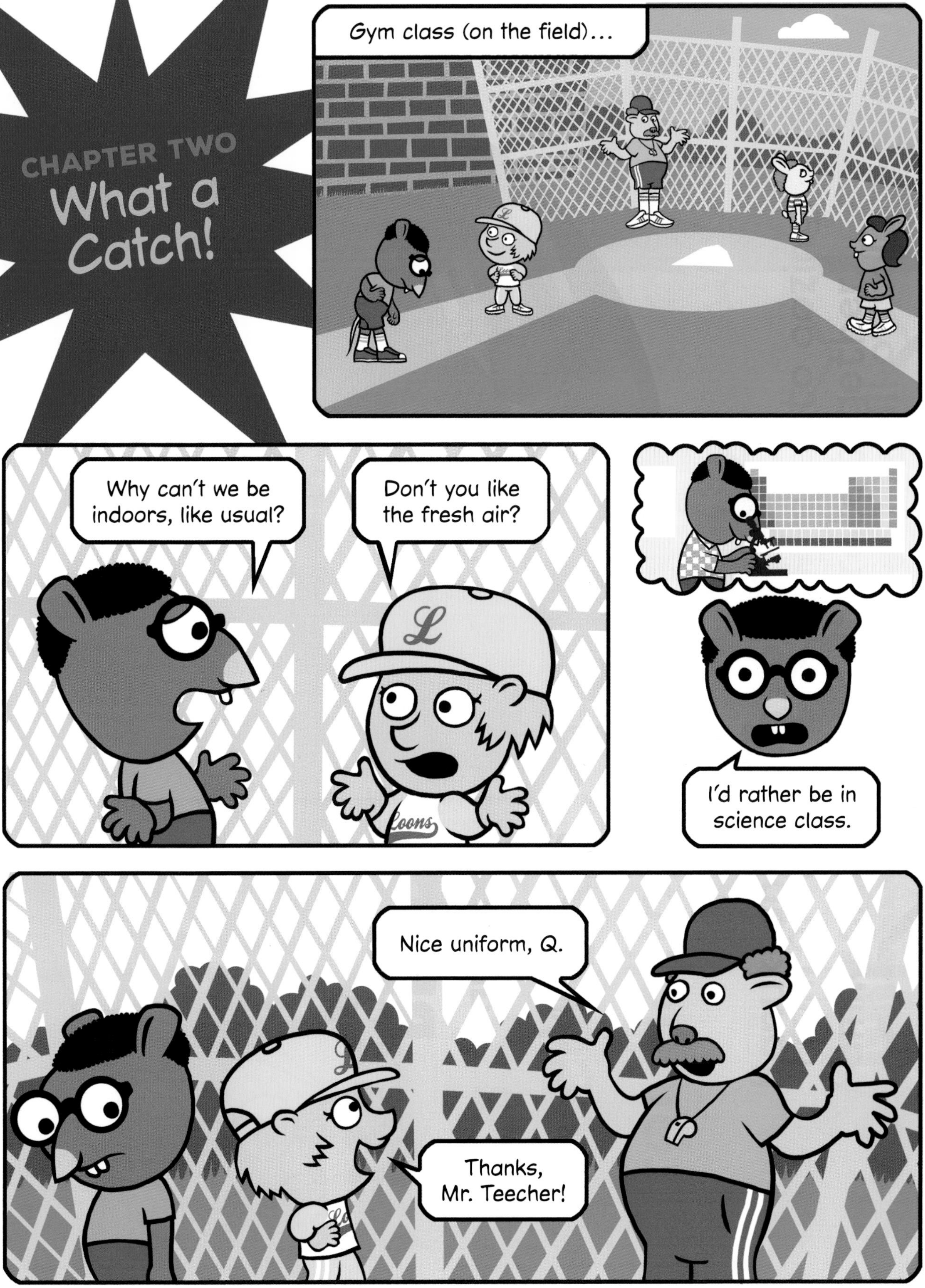
Gym class (on the field)...
Why can't we be indoors, like usual?
Don't you like the fresh air?
I'd rather be in science class.
Nice uniform, Q.
Thanks, Mr. Teecher!

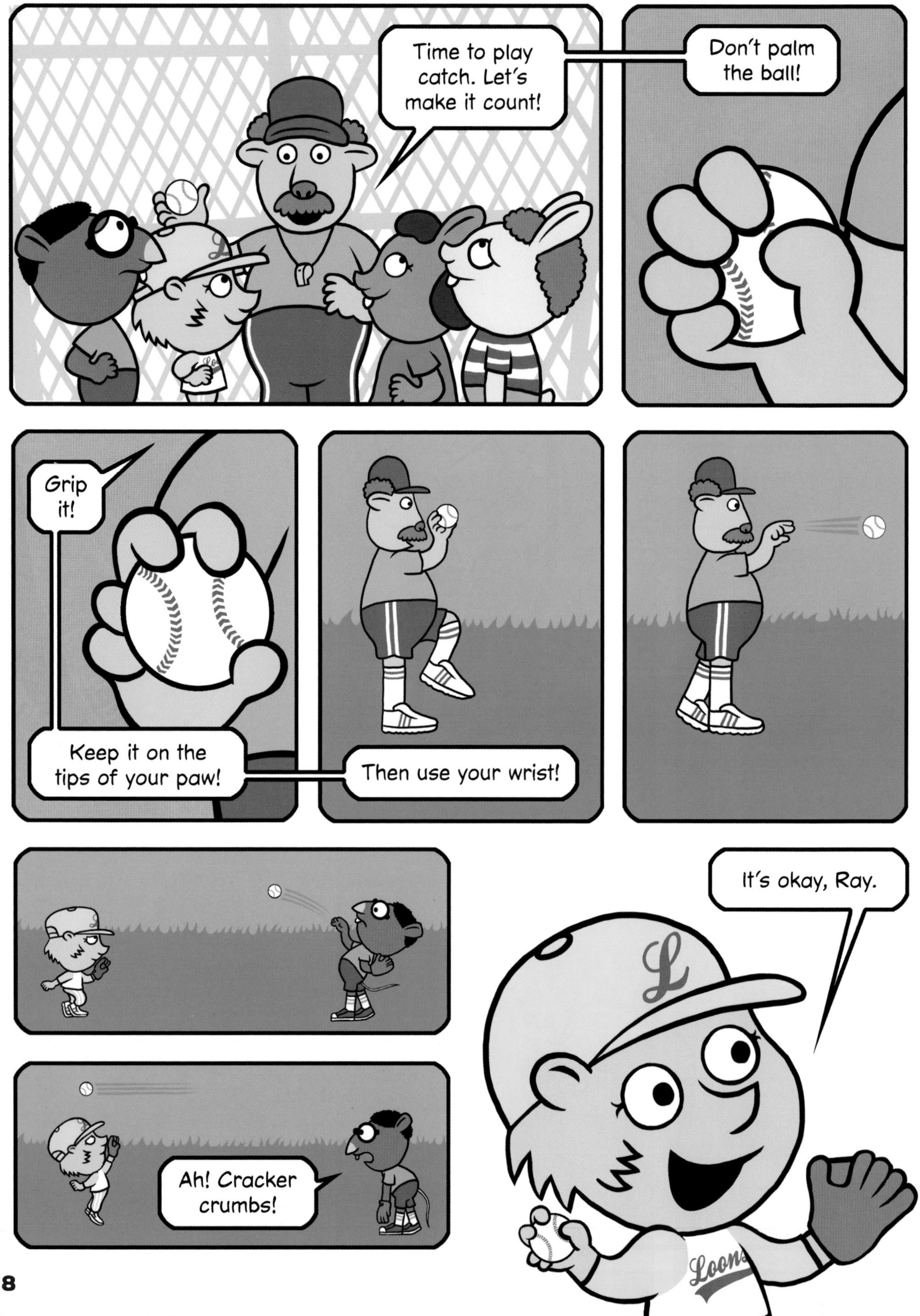
Time to play catch. Let's make it count!
Don't palm the ball!
Grip it!
Keep it on the tips of your paw!
Then use your wrist!
Ah! Cracker crumbs!
It's okay, Ray.

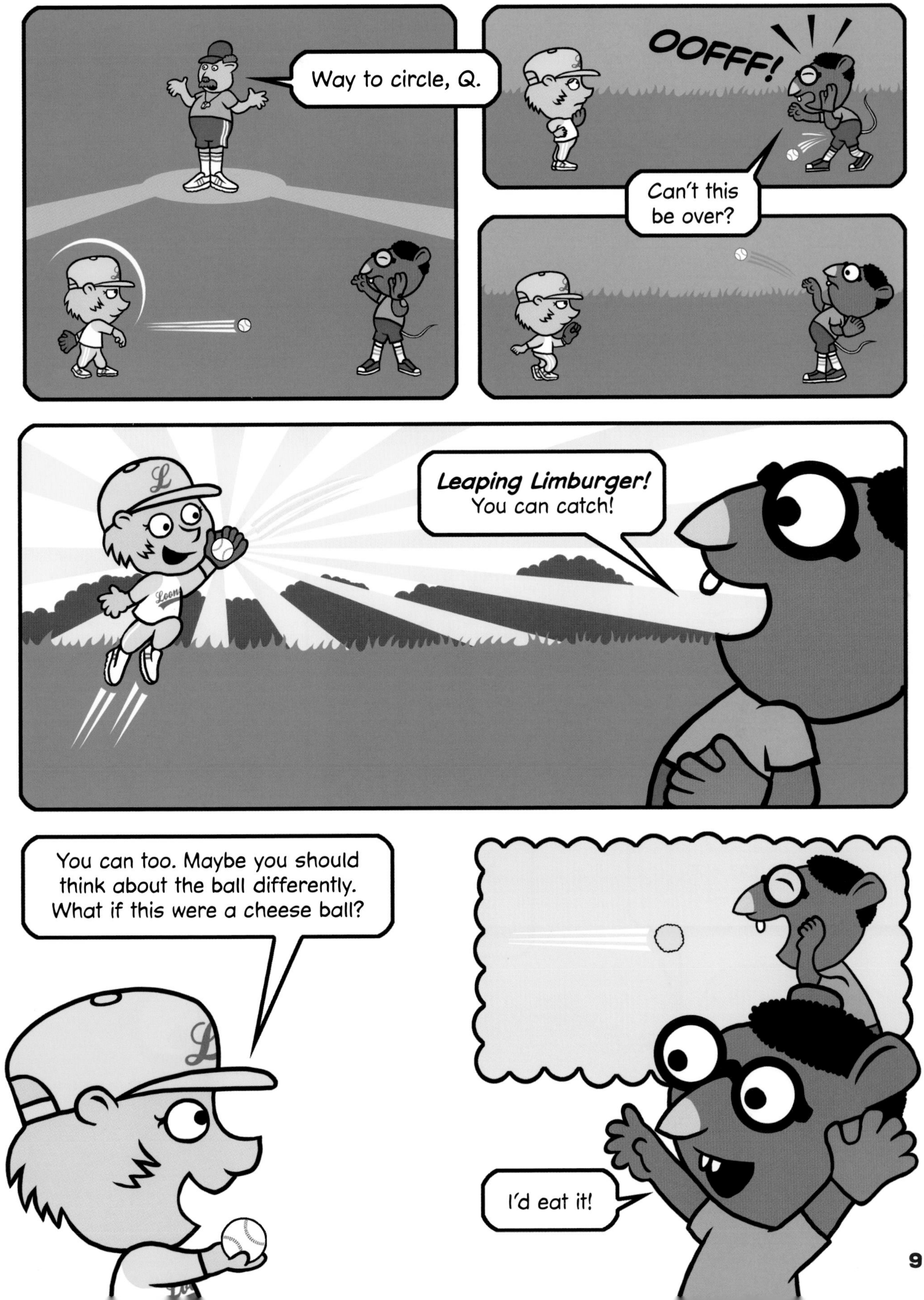

Way to circle, Q.
OOFFF!
Can't this be over?
Leaping Limburger! You can catch!
You can too. Maybe you should think about the ball differently. What if this were a cheese ball?
I'd eat it!

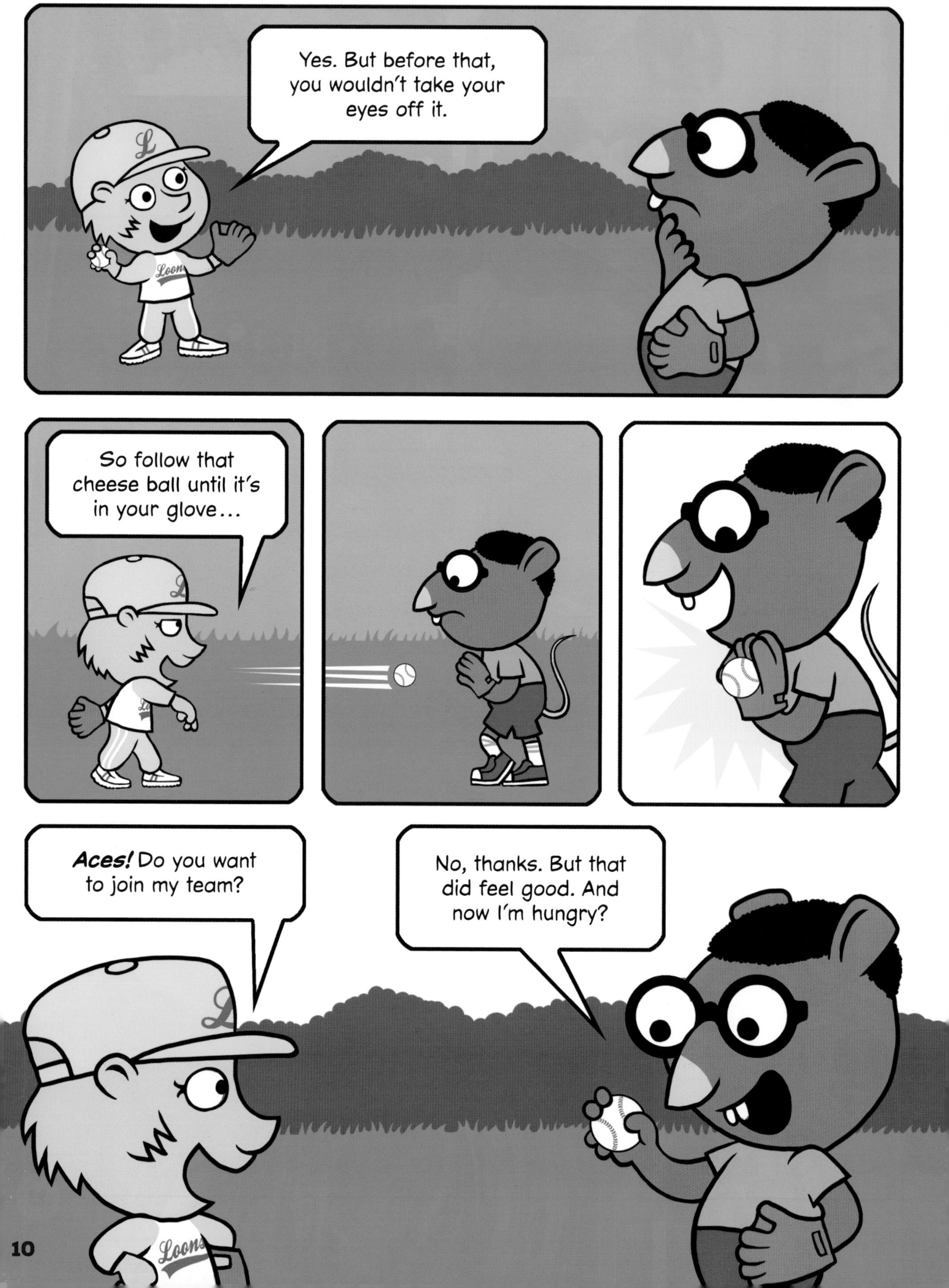

Yes. But before that, you wouldn't take your eyes off it.
So follow that cheese ball until it's in your glove...
Loons
Aces! Do you want to join my team?
No, thanks. But that did feel good. And now I'm hungry?
Loons

CHAPTER THREE
Pen Lifts and Ink Blots

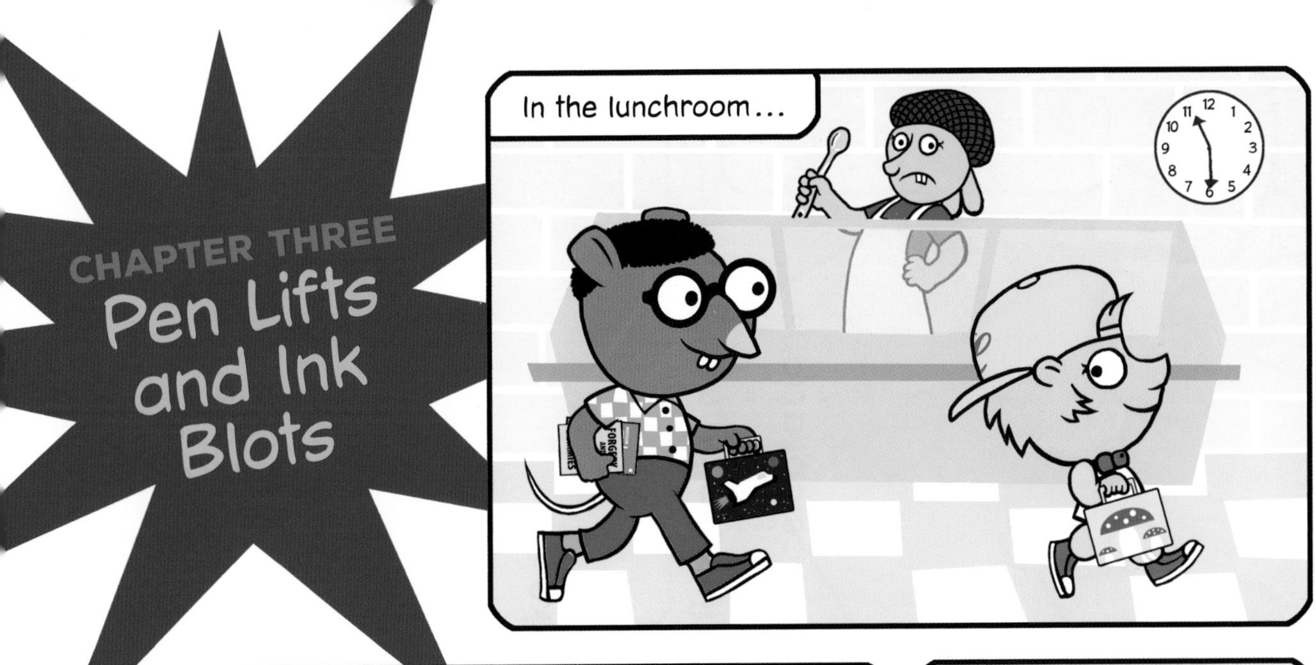
In the lunchroom . . .

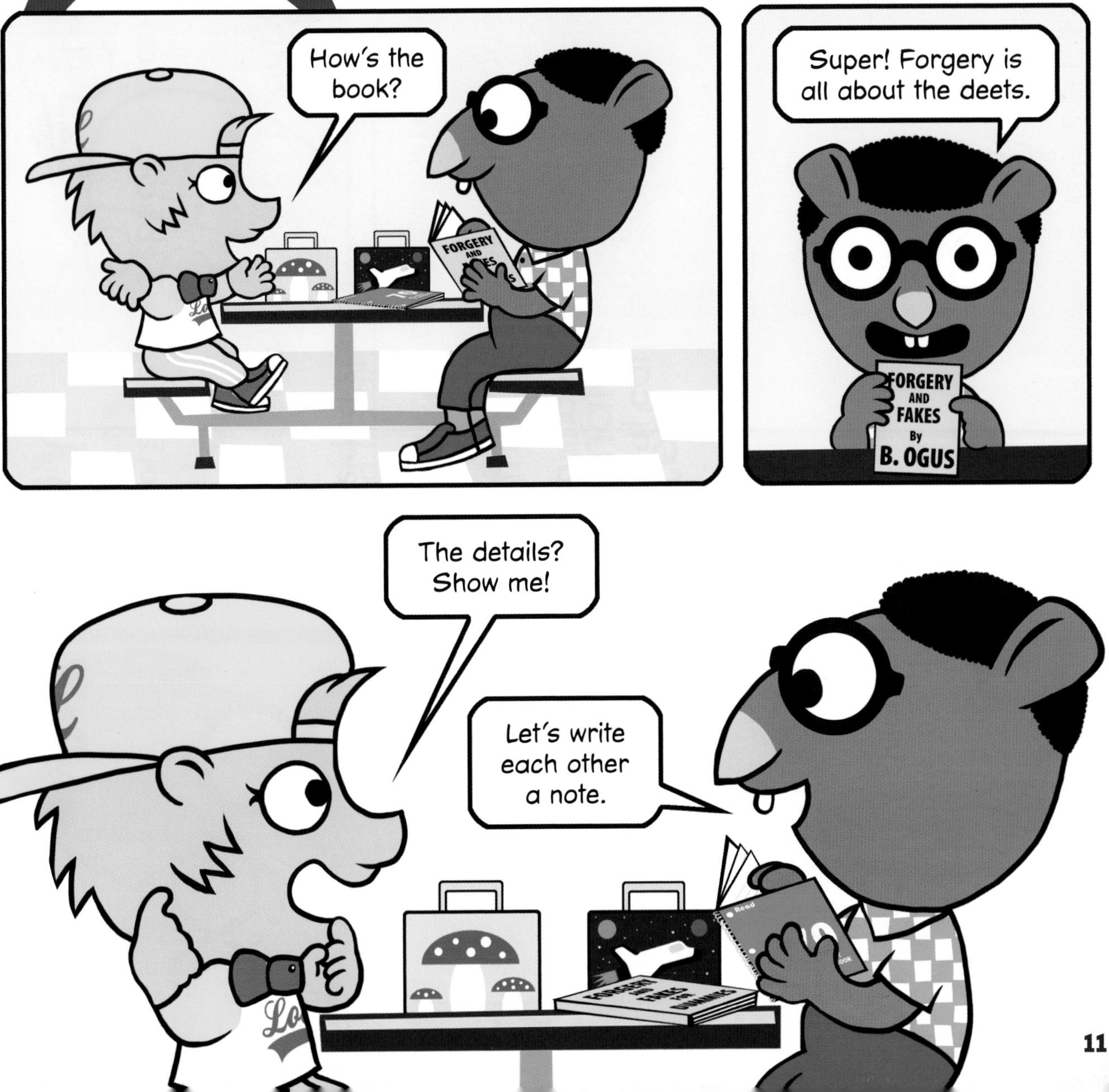
How's the book?
Super! Forgery is all about the deets.
FORGERY AND FAKES By B. OGUS
The details? Show me!
Let's write each other a note.

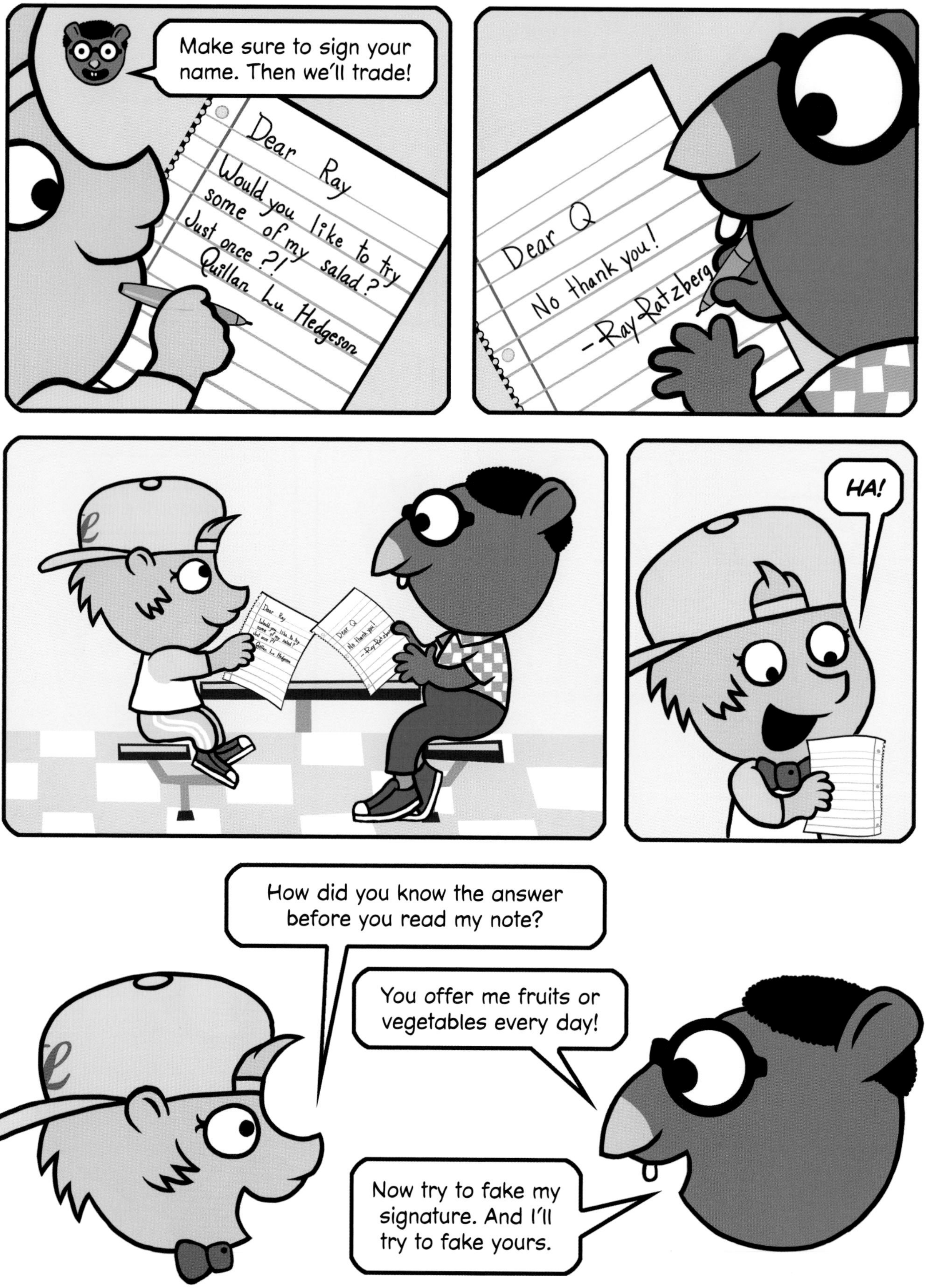
Make sure to sign your name. Then we'll trade!
Dear Ray
Would you like to try some of my salad? Just once?!
Quillan Lu Hedgeson
Dear Q
No thank you!
-Ray Ratzberg
HA!
How did you know the answer before you read my note?
You offer me fruits or vegetables every day!
Now try to fake my signature. And I'll try to fake yours.

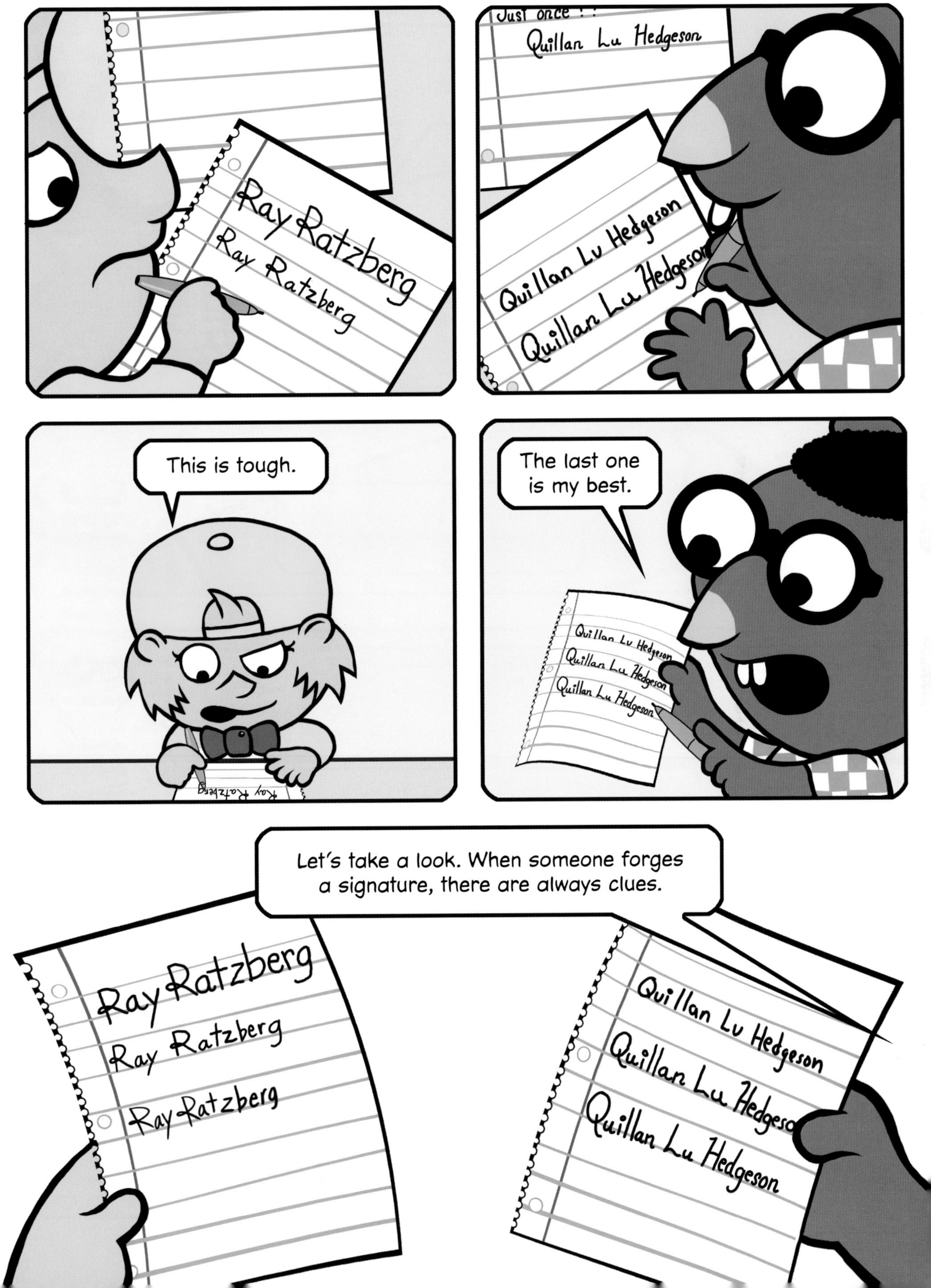

Just once . . .
Quillan Lu Hedgeson
Ray Ratzberg
Ray Ratzberg
Quillan Lu Hedgeson
Quillan Lu Hedgeson
This is tough.
The last one is my best.
Quillan Lu Hedgeson
Quillan Lu Hedgeson
Quillan Lu Hedgeson
Let's take a look. When someone forges a signature, there are always clues.
Ray Ratzberg
Ray Ratzberg
Ray Ratzberg
Quillan Lu Hedgeson
Quillan Lu Hedgeso
Quillan Lu Hedgeson

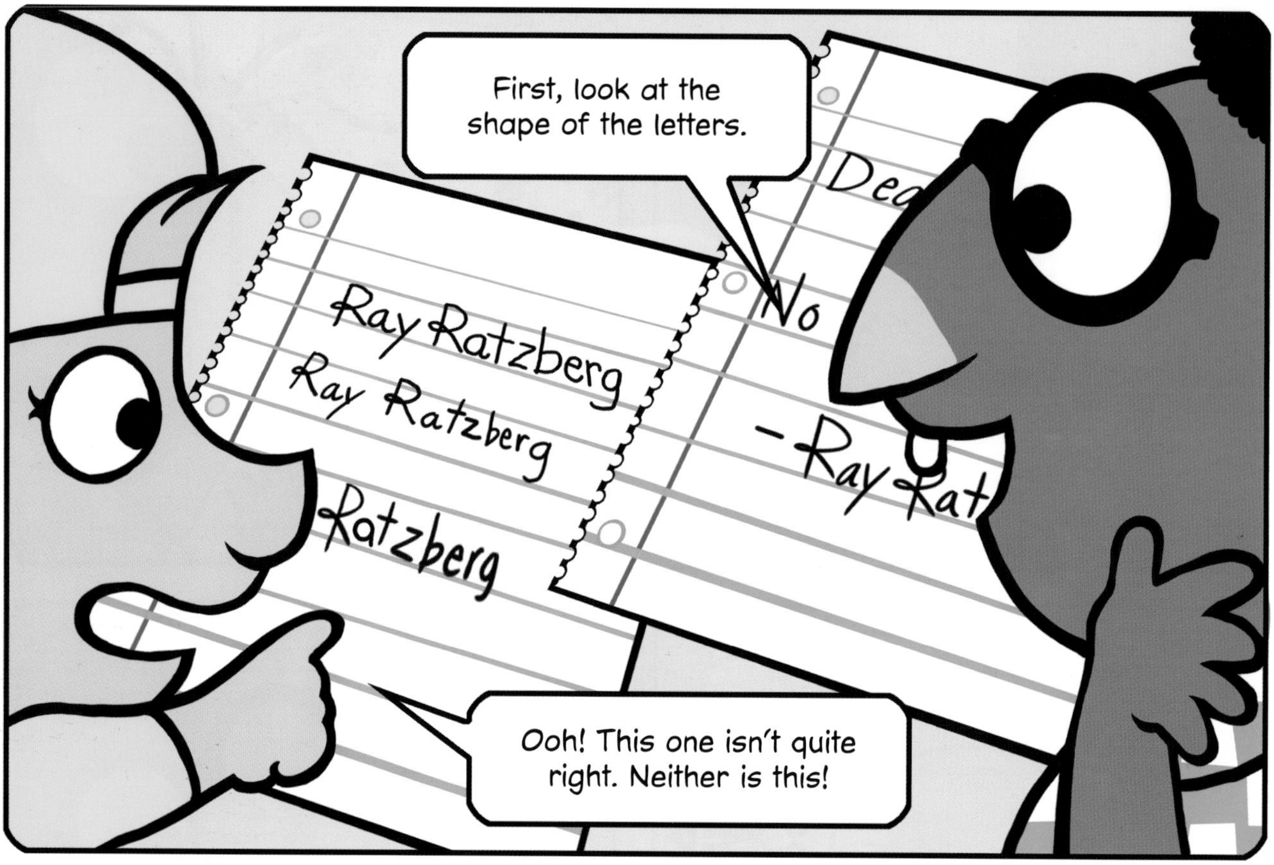
First, look at the shape of the letters.
Ooh! This one isn't quite right. Neither is this!

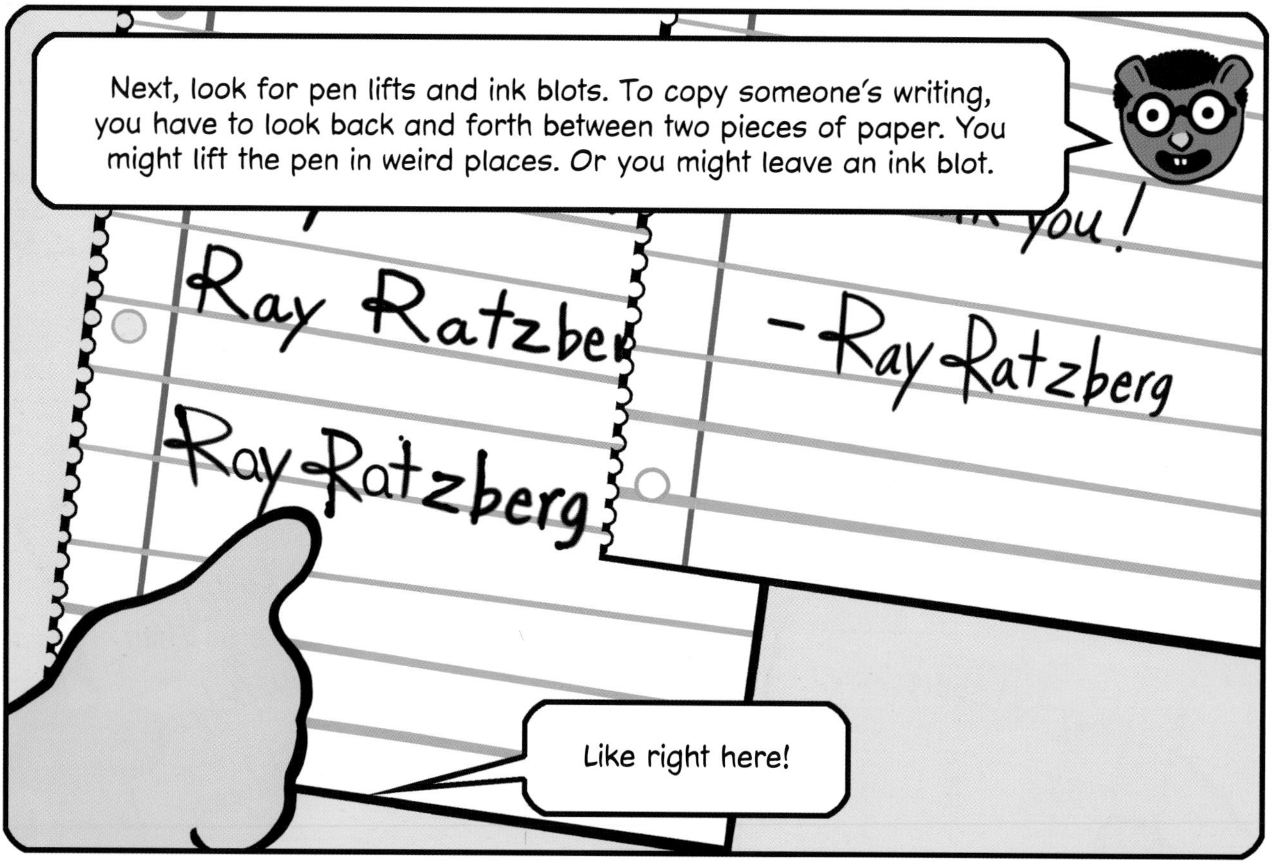
Next, look for pen lifts and ink blots. To copy someone's writing, you have to look back and forth between two pieces of paper. You might lift the pen in weird places. Or you might leave an ink blot.
Like right here!

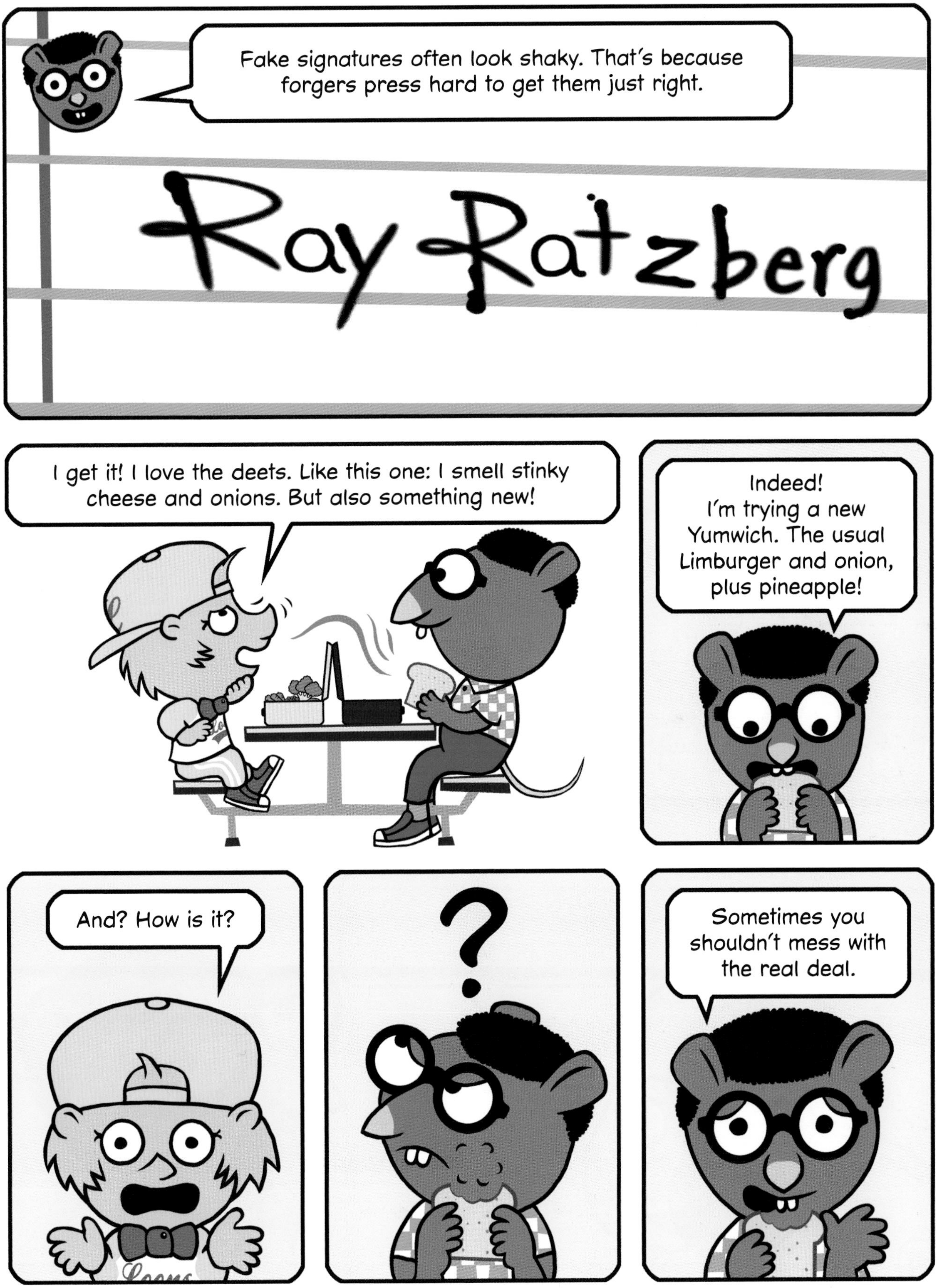

Fake signatures often look shaky. That's because forgers press hard to get them just right.
Ray Ratzberg
I get it! I love the deets. Like this one: I smell stinky cheese and onions. But also something new!
Indeed! I'm trying a new Yumwich. The usual Limburger and onion, plus pineapple!
And? How is it?
?
Sometimes you shouldn't mess with the real deal.

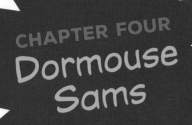

CHAPTER FOUR
Dormouse Sams

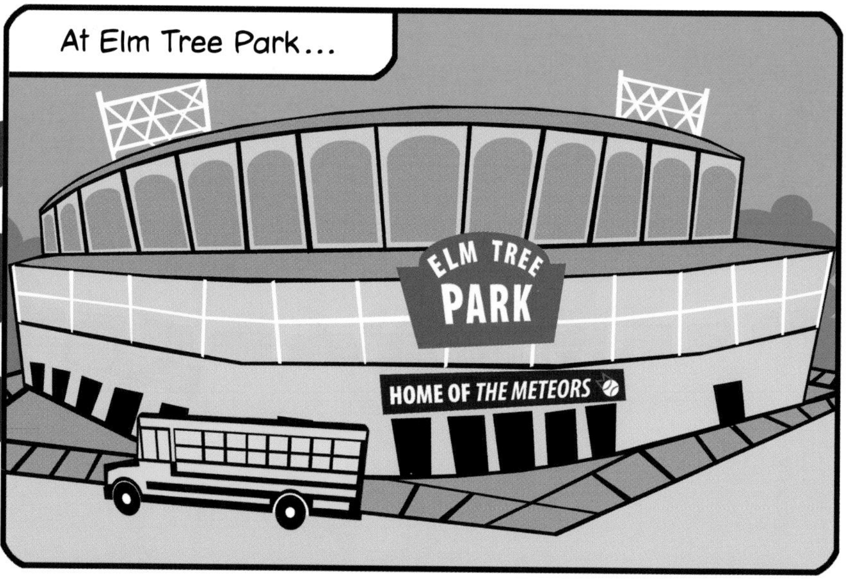
At Elm Tree Park...
ELM TREE PARK
HOME OF THE METEORS

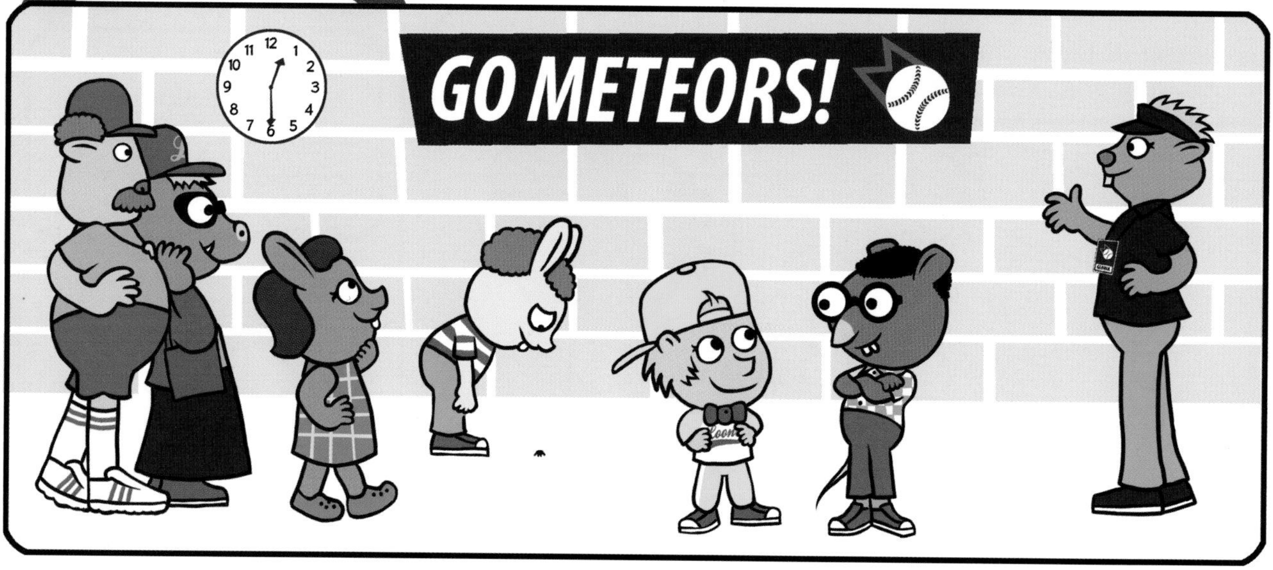
GO METEORS!

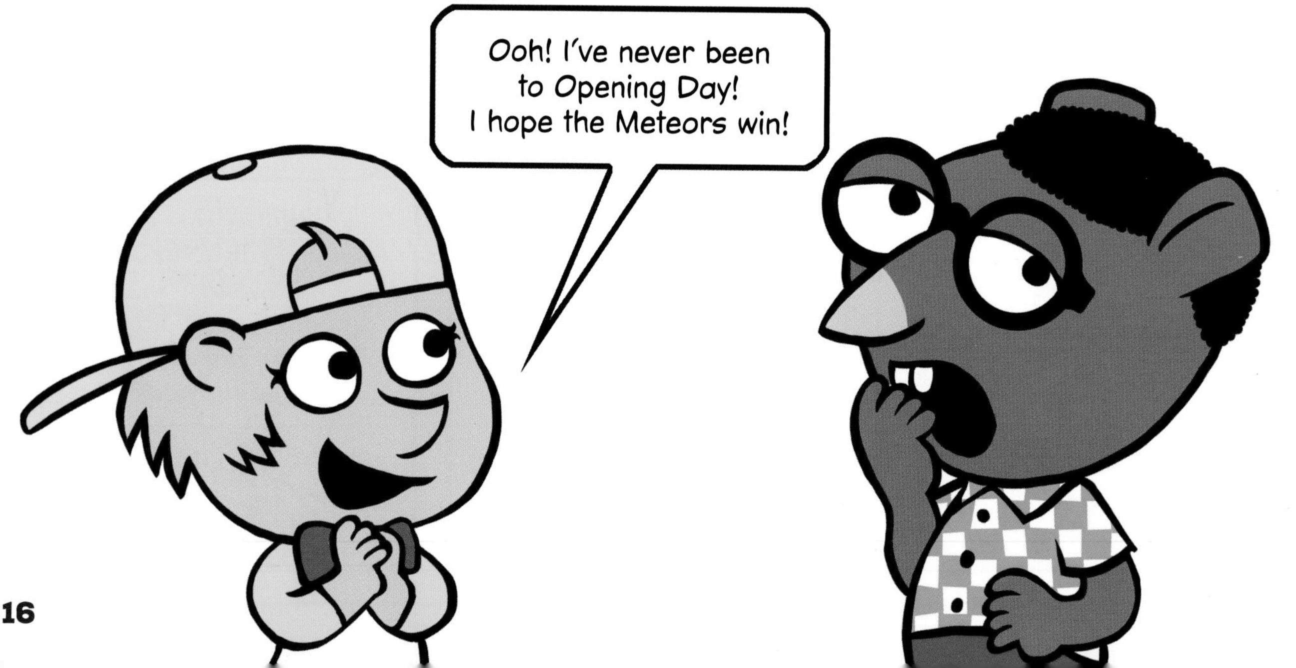
Ooh! I've never been to Opening Day! I hope the Meteors win!

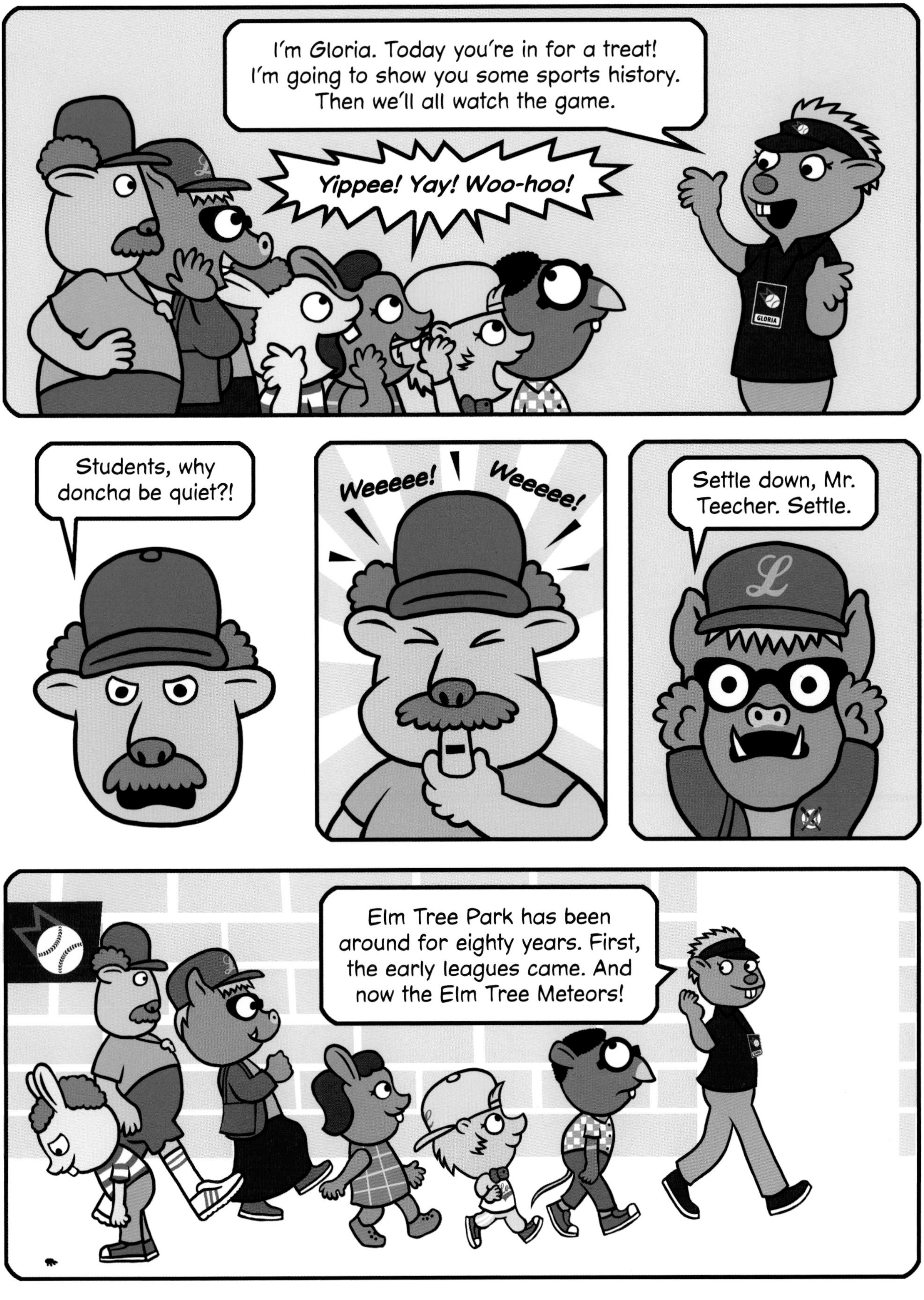
I'm Gloria. Today you're in for a treat! I'm going to show you some sports history. Then we'll all watch the game.
Yippee! Yay! Woo-hoo!
Students, why doncha be quiet?!
Weeeee! Weeeee!
Settle down, Mr. Teecher. Settle.
Elm Tree Park has been around for eighty years. First, the early leagues came. And now the Elm Tree Meteors!

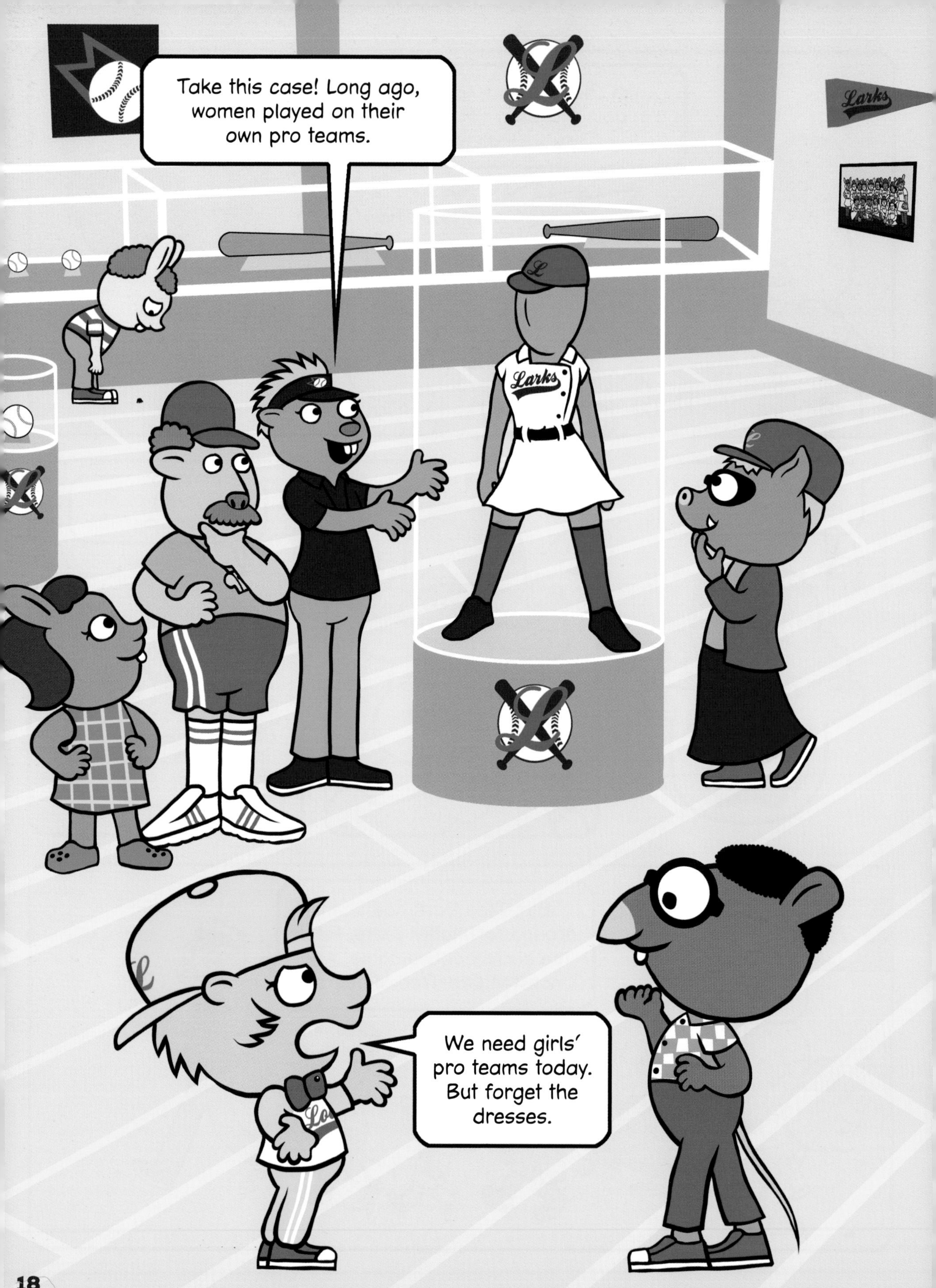
Larks
Larks
Take this case! Long ago, women played on their own pro teams.
We need girls' pro teams today. But forget the dresses.

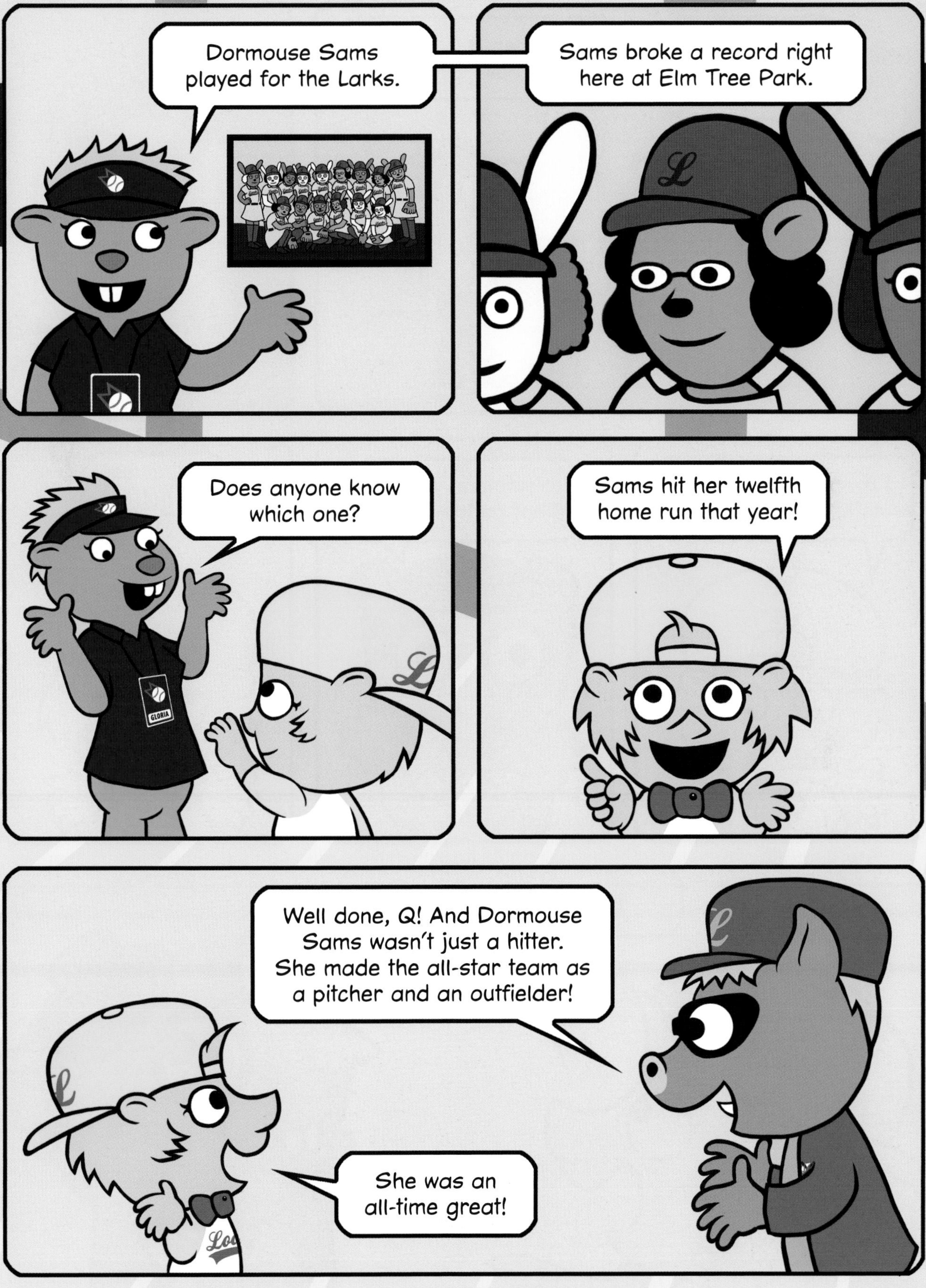
Dormouse Sams played for the Larks.
Sams broke a record right here at Elm Tree Park.
Does anyone know which one?
Sams hit her twelfth home run that year!
Well done, Q! And Dormouse Sams wasn't just a hitter. She made the all-star team as a pitcher and an outfielder!
She was an all-time great!

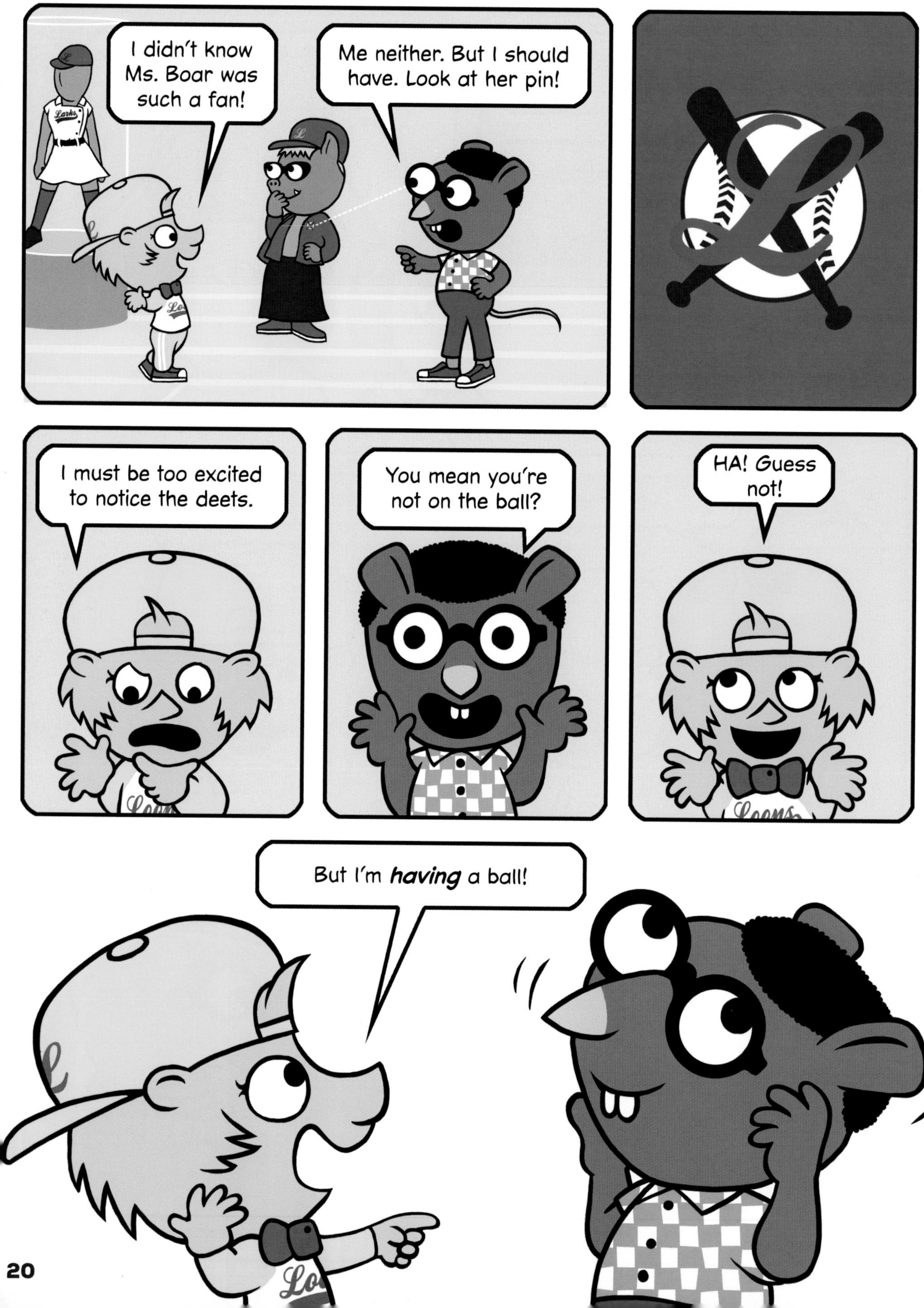
I didn't know Ms. Boar was such a fan!
Me neither. But I should have. Look at her pin!
Larks
I must be too excited to notice the deets.
You mean you're not on the ball?
HA! Guess not!
But I'm ***having*** a ball!

CHAPTER FIVE
Forged!

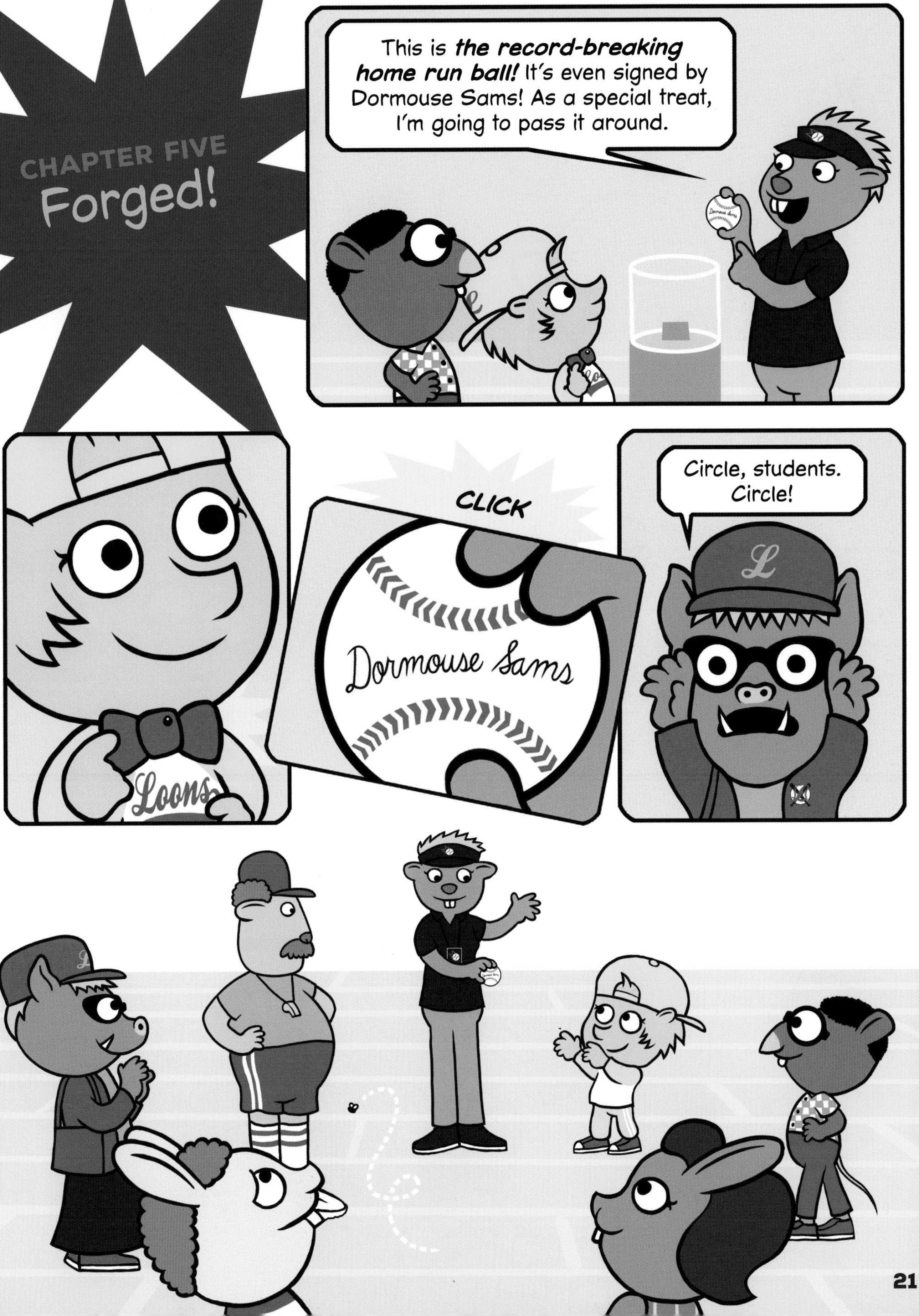
This is ***the record-breaking home run ball!*** It's even signed by Dormouse Sams! As a special treat, I'm going to pass it around.
Loons
CLICK
Dormouse Sams
Circle, students. Circle!

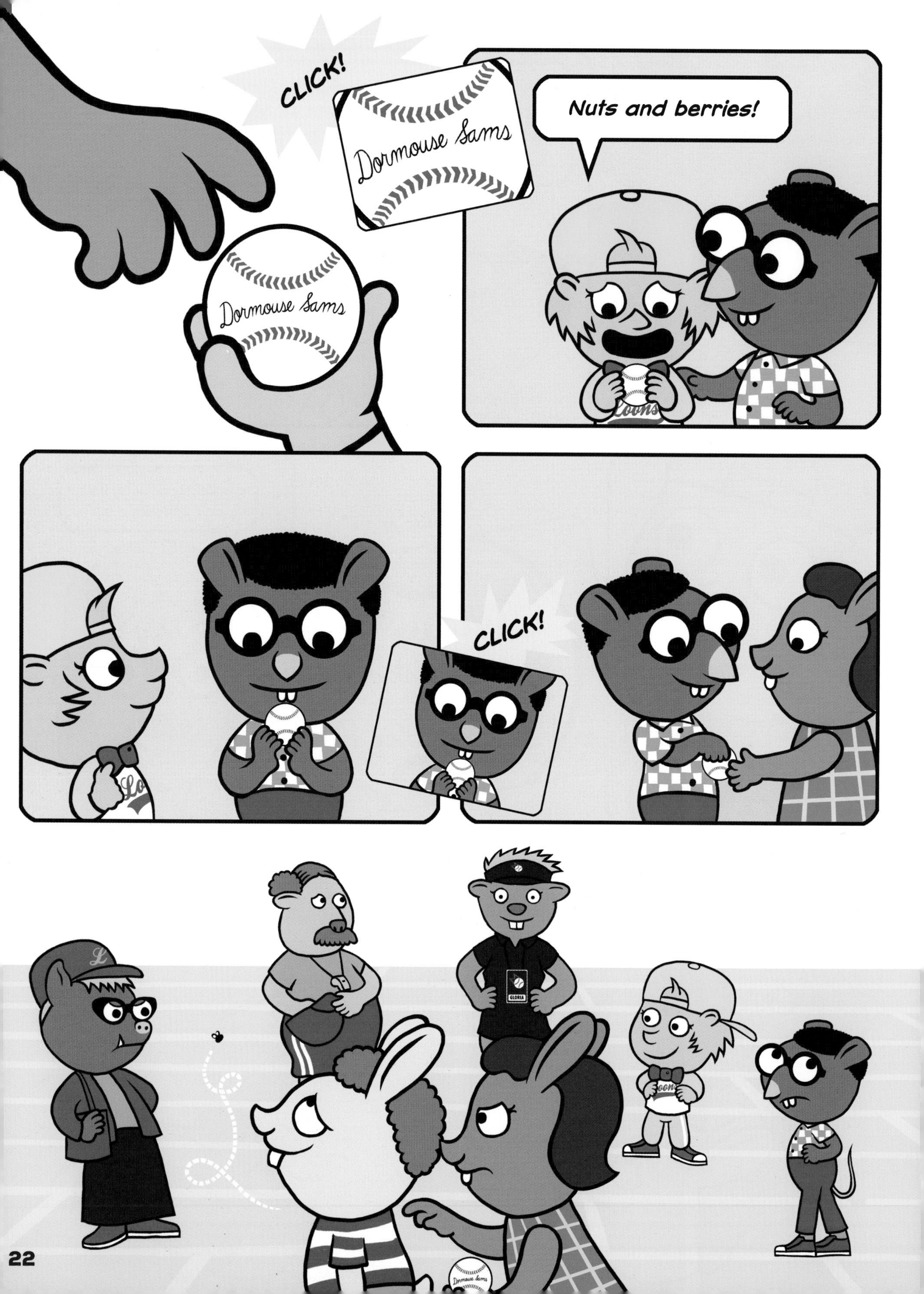
CLICK!
Dormouse Sams
Dormouse Sams
Nuts and berries!
Loons
CLICK!
GLORIA
Dormouse Sams

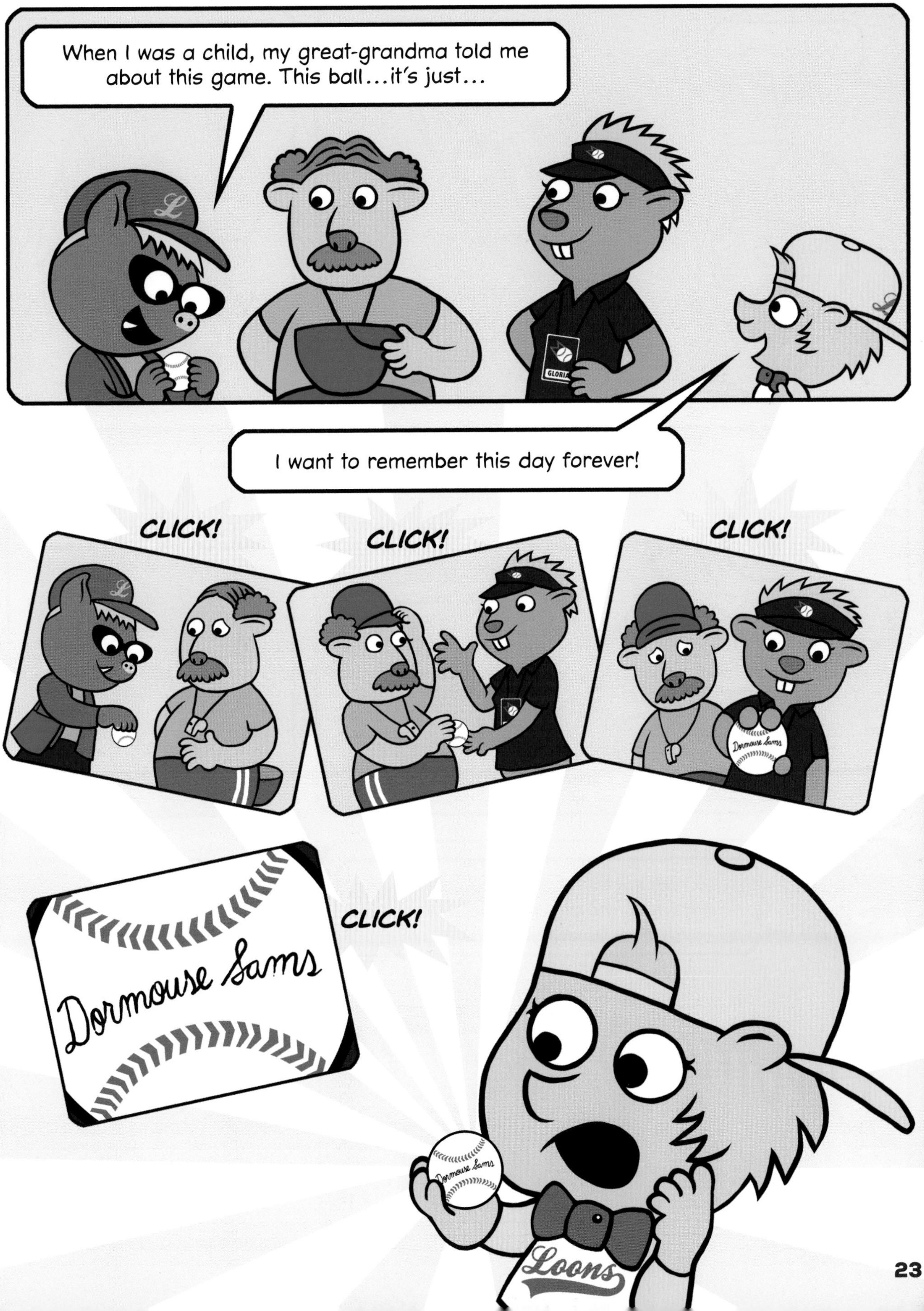

When I was a child, my great-grandma told me about this game. This ball...it's just...
GLORIA
I want to remember this day forever!
CLICK!
CLICK!
CLICK!
Dormouse Sams
Dormouse Sams
CLICK!
Dormouse Sams
Loons

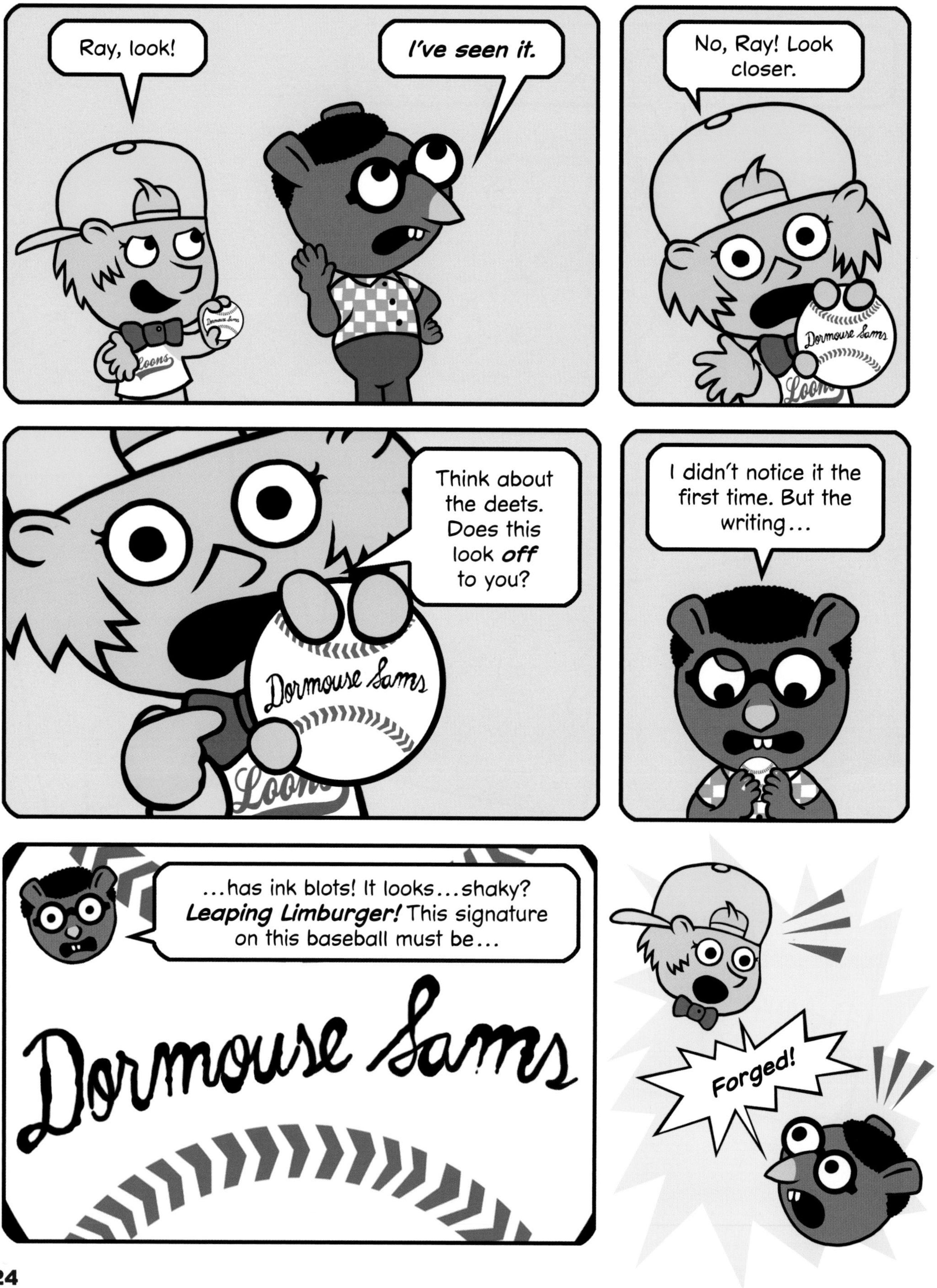

Ray, look!
I've seen it.
Dormouse Sams
Loons
No, Ray! Look closer.
Dormouse Sams
Loons
Think about the deets. Does this look off to you?
Dormouse Sams
Loons
I didn't notice it the first time. But the writing...
...has ink blots! It looks...shaky? Leaping Limburger! This signature on this baseball must be...
Dormouse Sams
Forged!

CHAPTER SIX
Time to Investigate

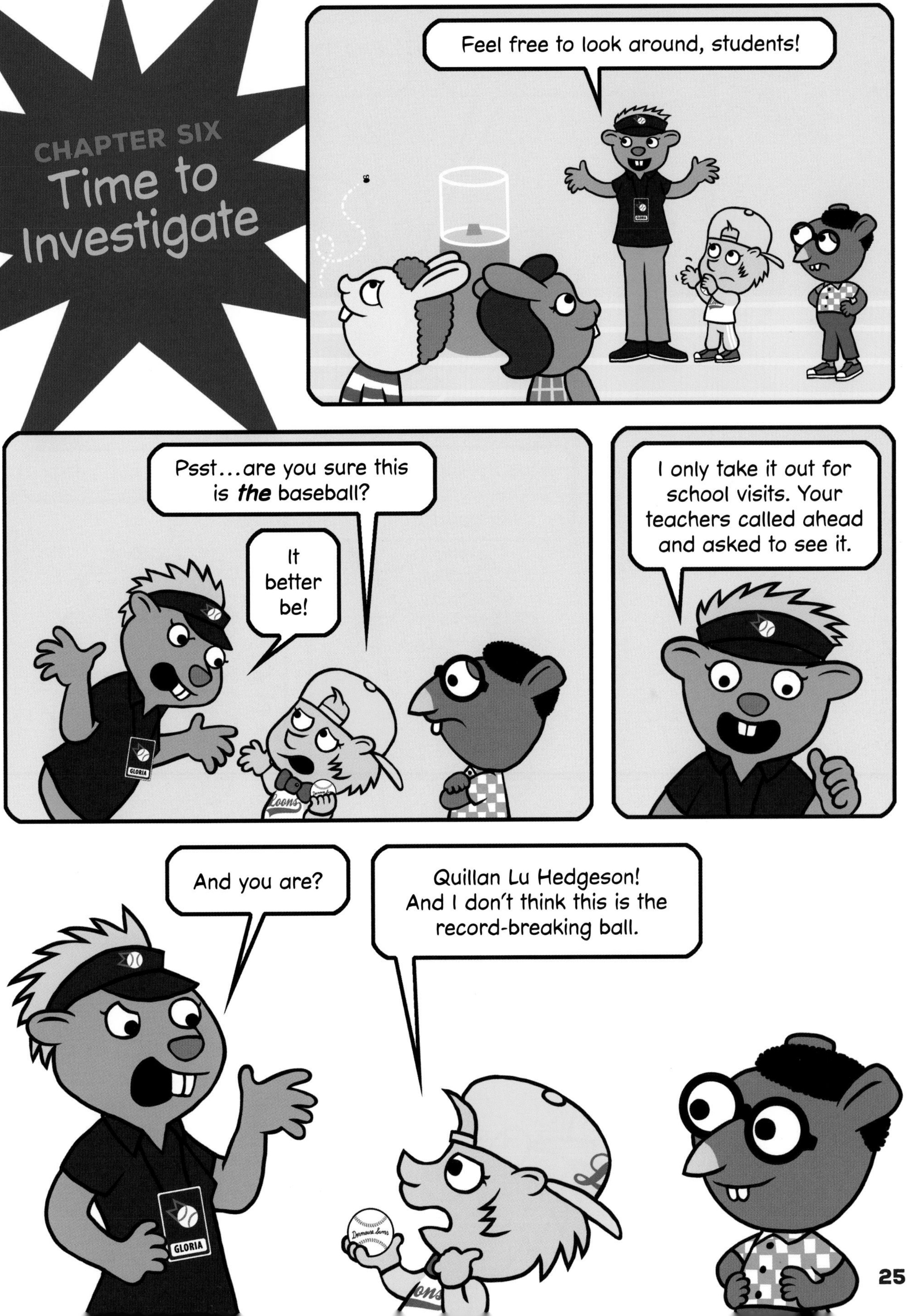

Feel free to look around, students!
GLORIA
Psst...are you sure this is *the* baseball?
It better be!
GLORIA
I only take it out for school visits. Your teachers called ahead and asked to see it.
And you are?
Quillan Lu Hedgeson! And I don't think this is the record-breaking ball.
GLORIA

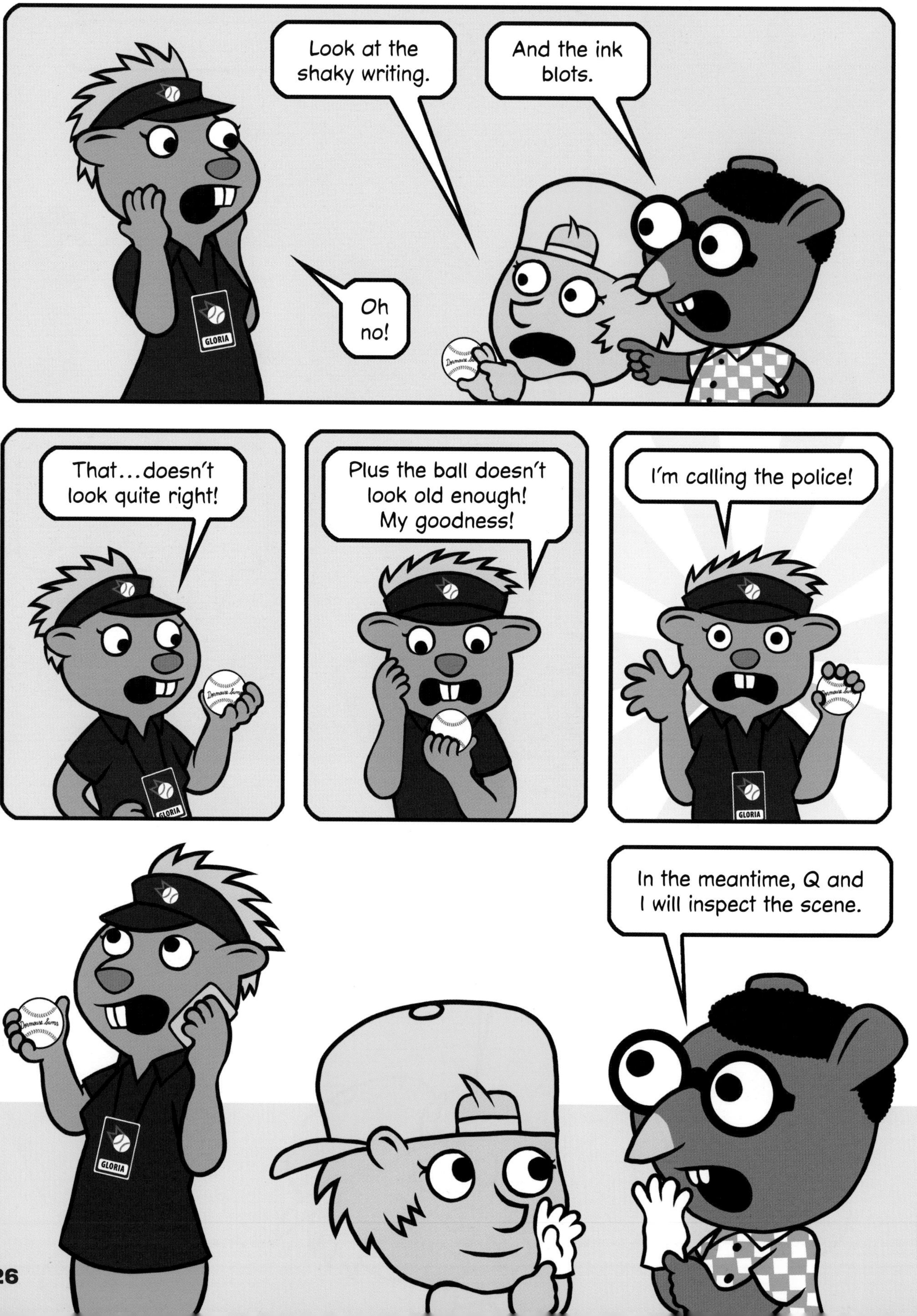

Look at the shaky writing.
And the ink blots.
Oh no!
GLORIA
That...doesn't look quite right!
Plus the ball doesn't look old enough! My goodness!
I'm calling the police!
In the meantime, Q and I will inspect the scene.

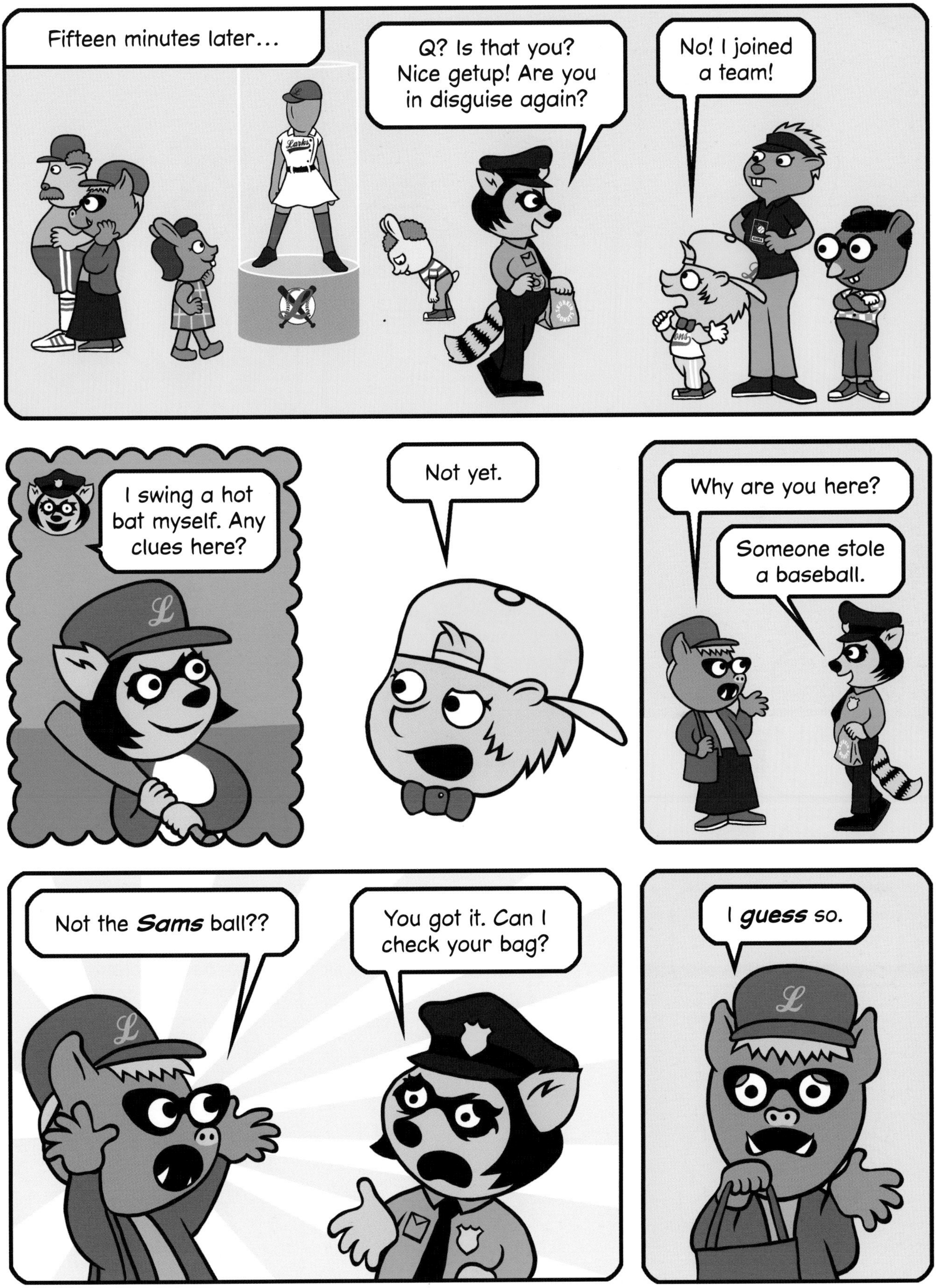

Fifteen minutes later...
Q? Is that you? Nice getup! Are you in disguise again?
No! I joined a team!
I swing a hot bat myself. Any clues here?
Not yet.
Why are you here?
Someone stole a baseball.
Not the *Sams* ball??
You got it. Can I check your bag?
I *guess* so.

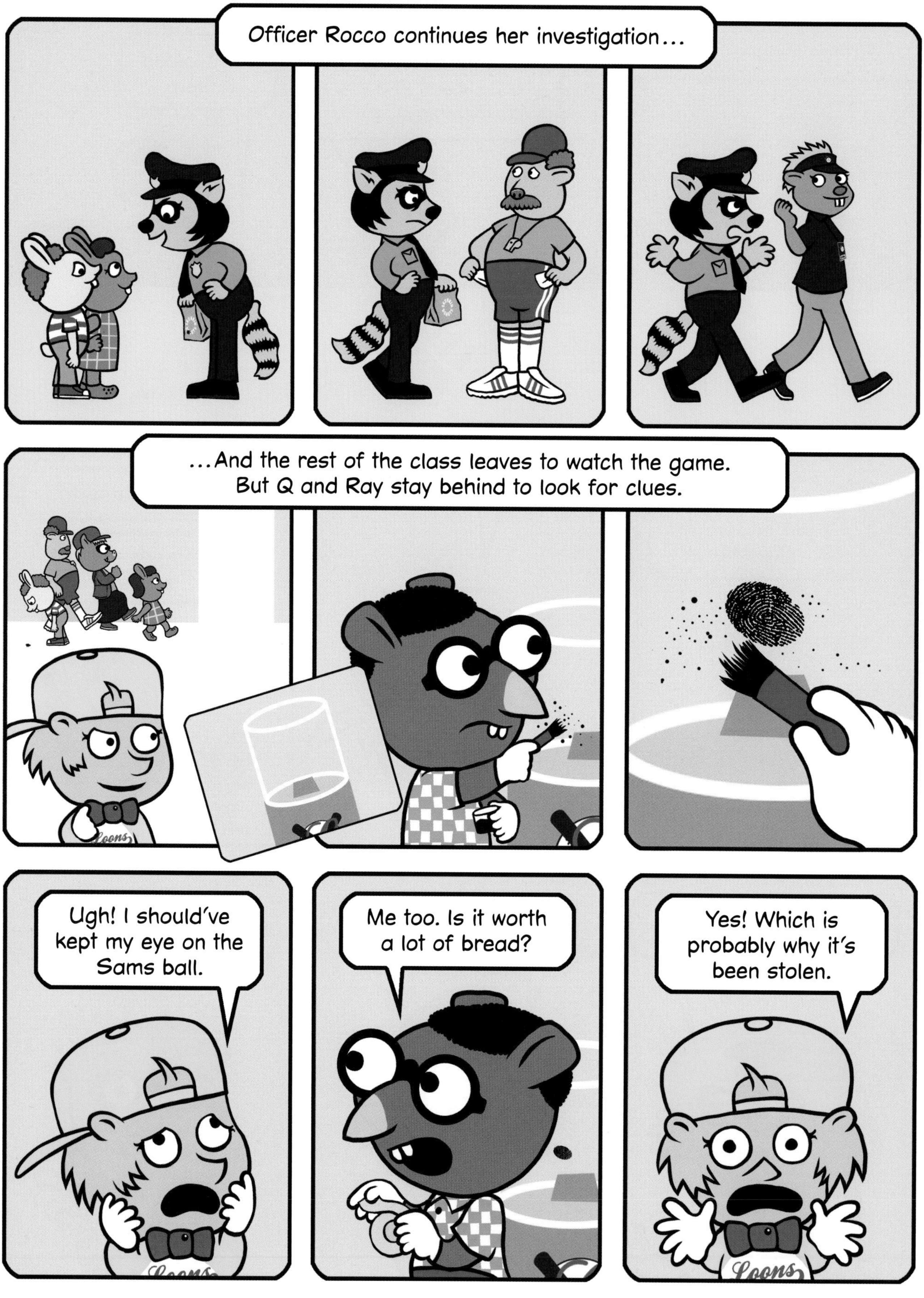
Officer Rocco continues her investigation...
...And the rest of the class leaves to watch the game. But Q and Ray stay behind to look for clues.
Ugh! I should've kept my eye on the Sams ball.
Me too. Is it worth a lot of bread?
Yes! Which is probably why it's been stolen.

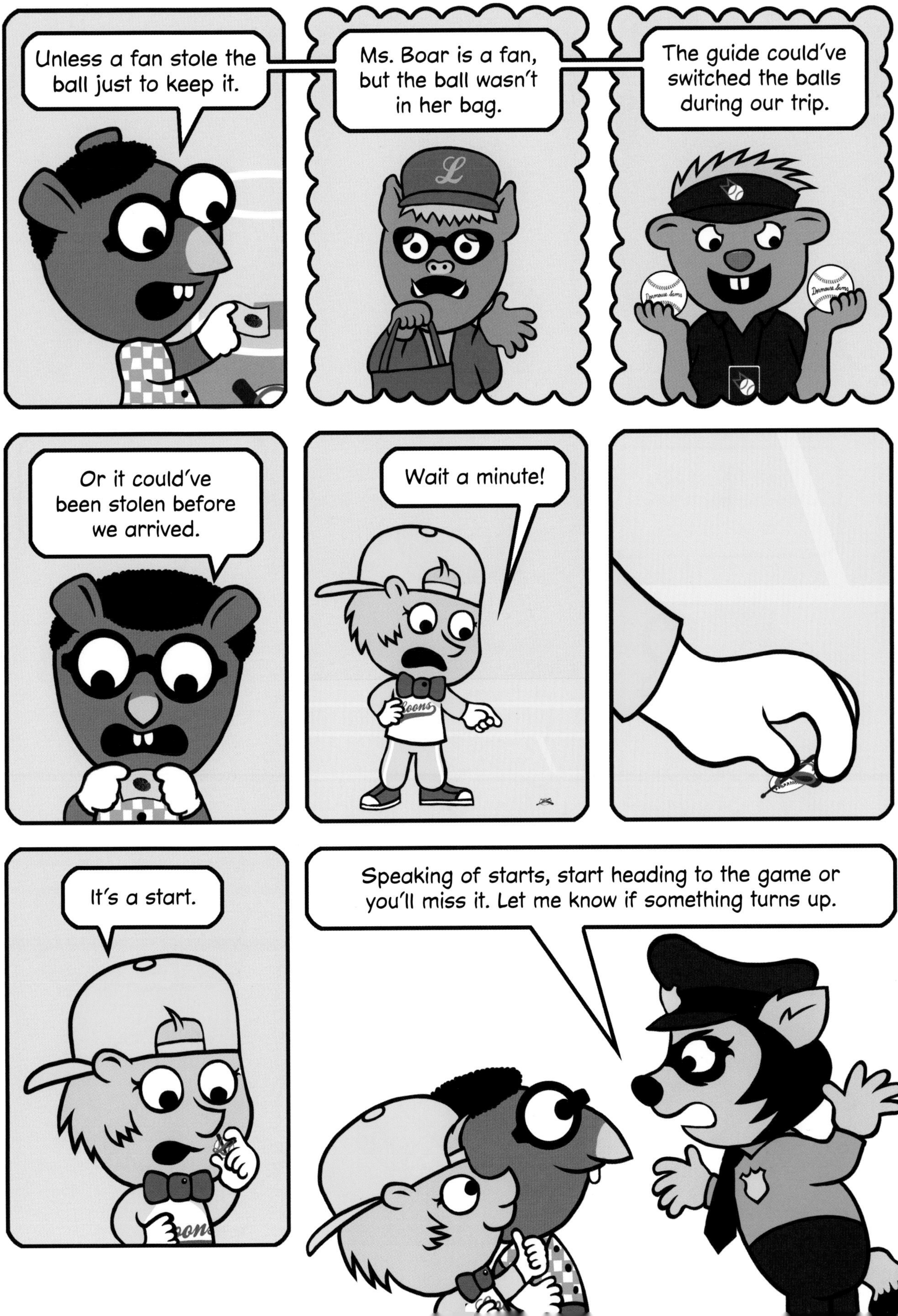

Unless a fan stole the ball just to keep it.
Ms. Boar is a fan, but the ball wasn't in her bag.
The guide could've switched the balls during our trip.
Or it could've been stolen before we arrived.
Wait a minute!
It's a start.
Speaking of starts, start heading to the game or you'll miss it. Let me know if something turns up.

CHAPTER SEVEN
Collecting Clues

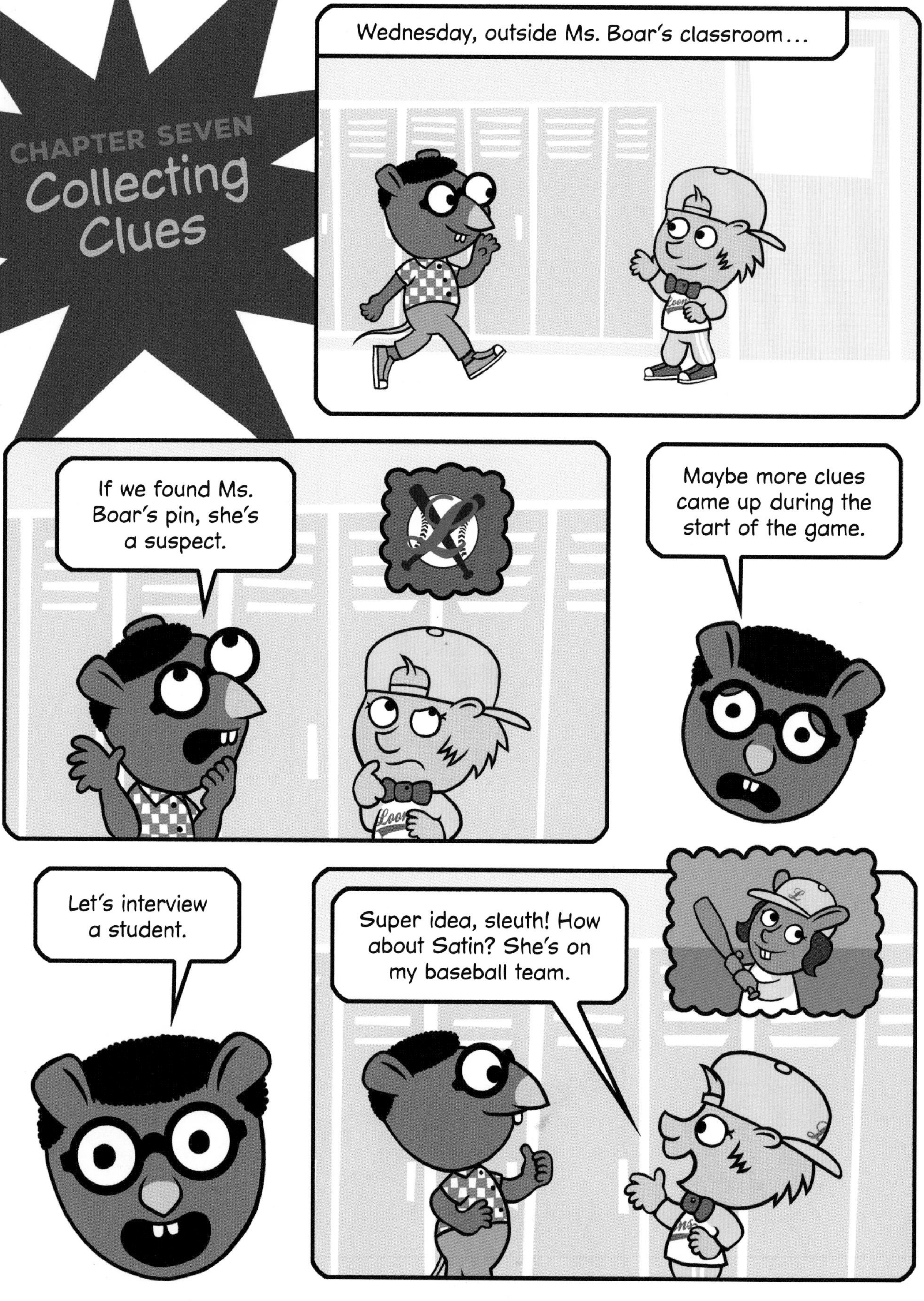

Wednesday, outside Ms. Boar's classroom...
If we found Ms. Boar's pin, she's a suspect.
Maybe more clues came up during the start of the game.
Let's interview a student.
Super idea, sleuth! How about Satin? She's on my baseball team.

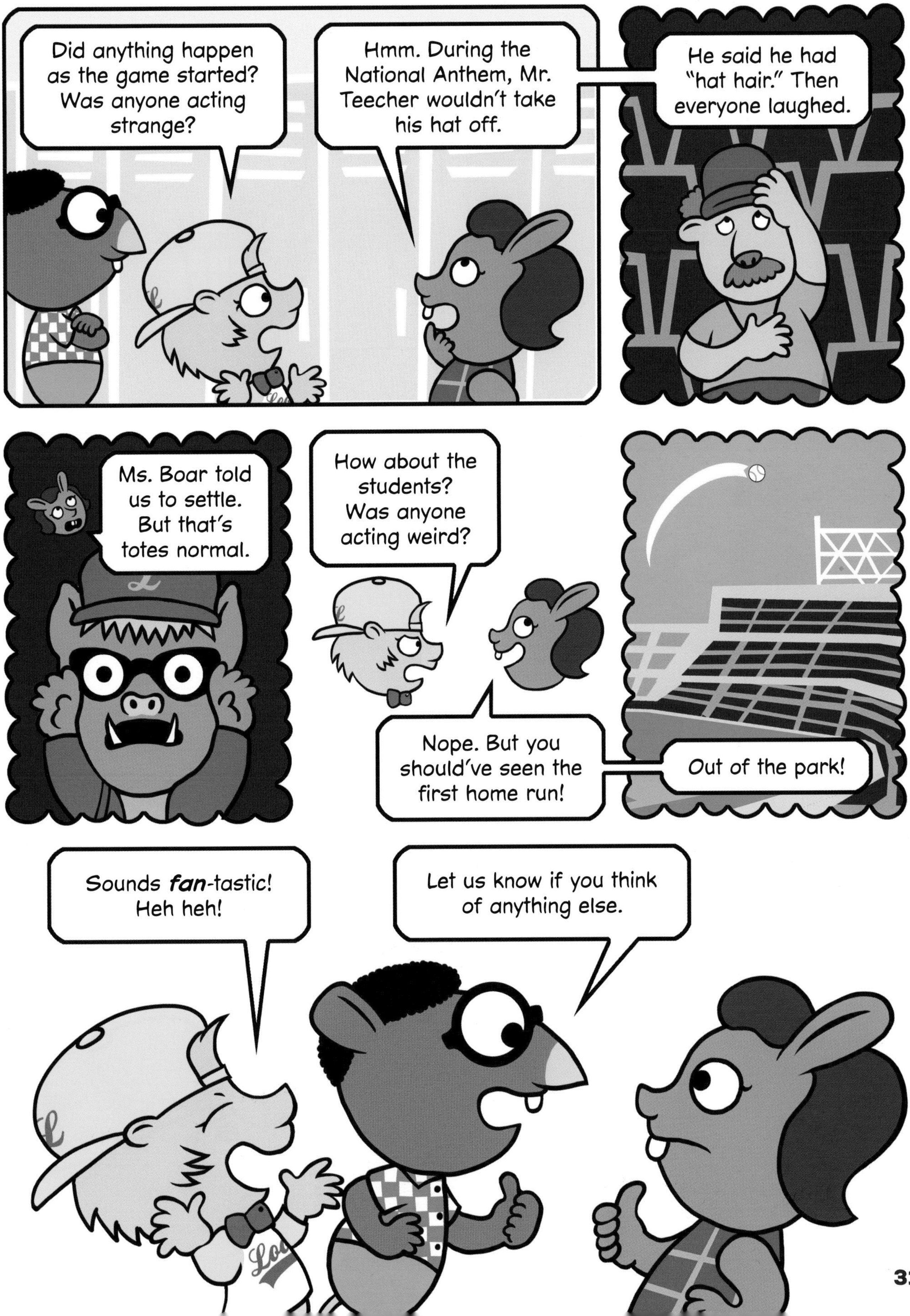
Did anything happen as the game started? Was anyone acting strange?
Hmm. During the National Anthem, Mr. Teecher wouldn't take his hat off.
He said he had "hat hair." Then everyone laughed.
Ms. Boar told us to settle. But that's totes normal.
How about the students? Was anyone acting weird?
Nope. But you should've seen the first home run!
Out of the park!
Sounds ***fan***-tastic! Heh heh!
Let us know if you think of anything else.

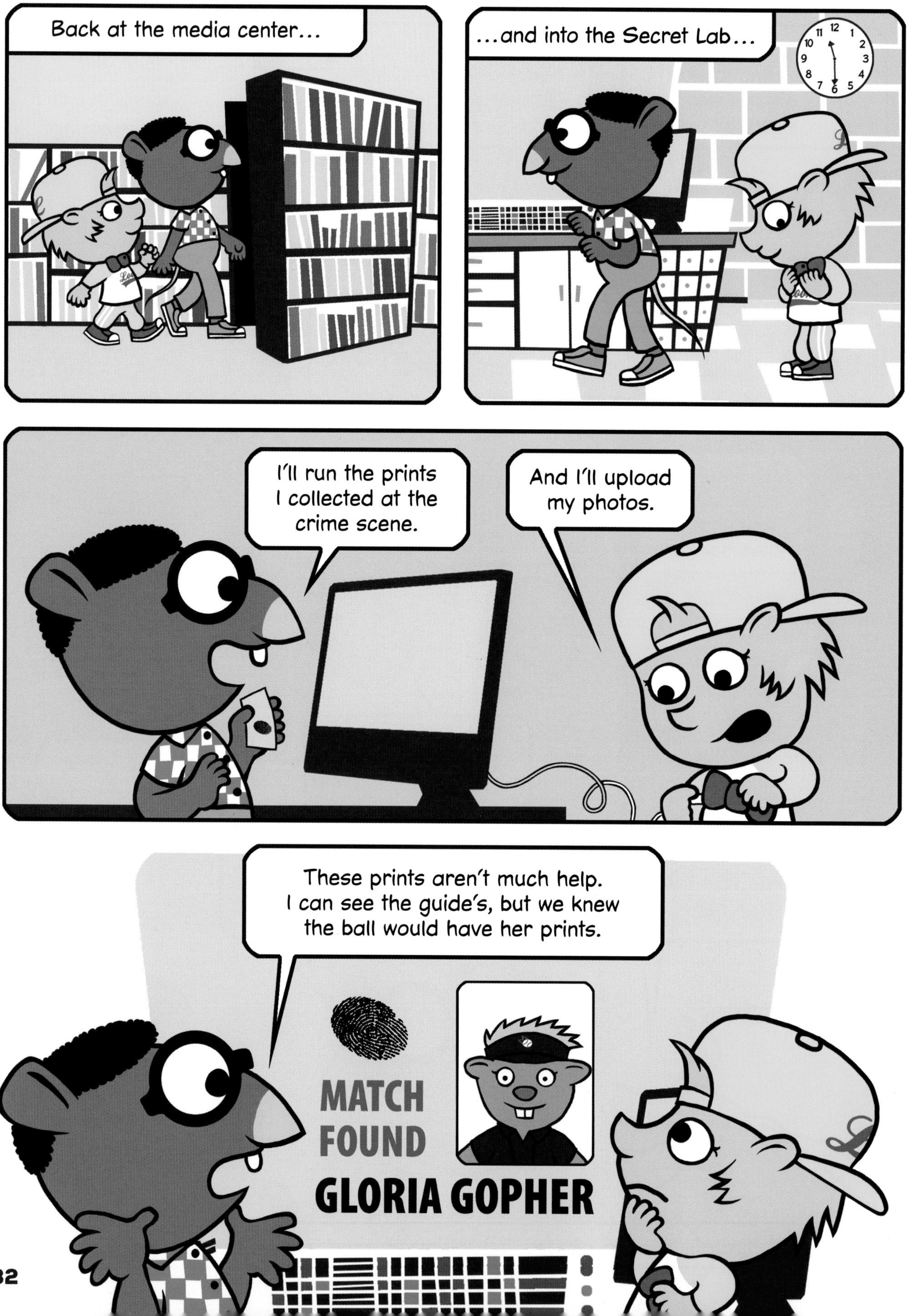
Back at the media center...
...and into the Secret Lab...
I'll run the prints I collected at the crime scene.
And I'll upload my photos.
These prints aren't much help. I can see the guide's, but we knew the ball would have her prints.
MATCH FOUND
GLORIA GOPHER

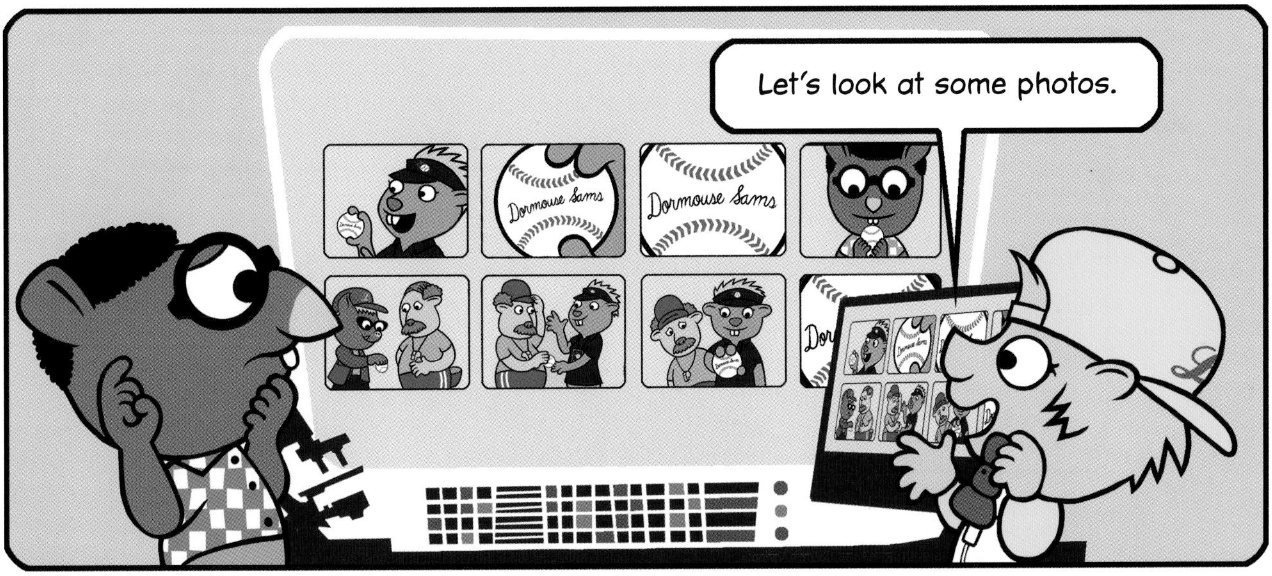
Let's look at some photos.

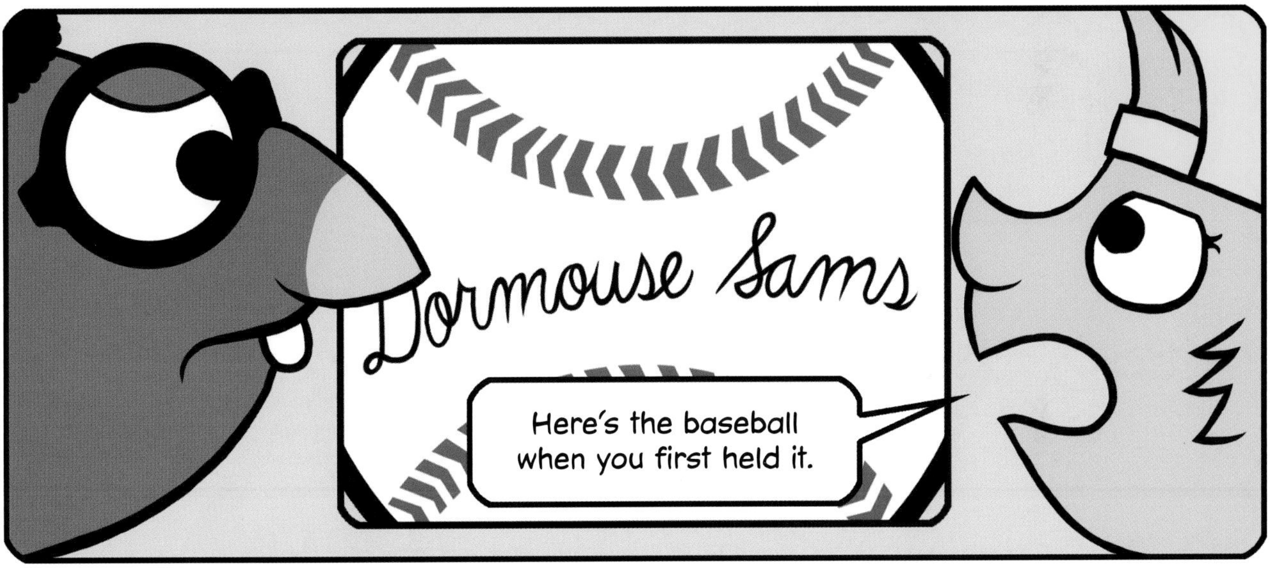
Dormouse Sams
Here's the baseball when you first held it.

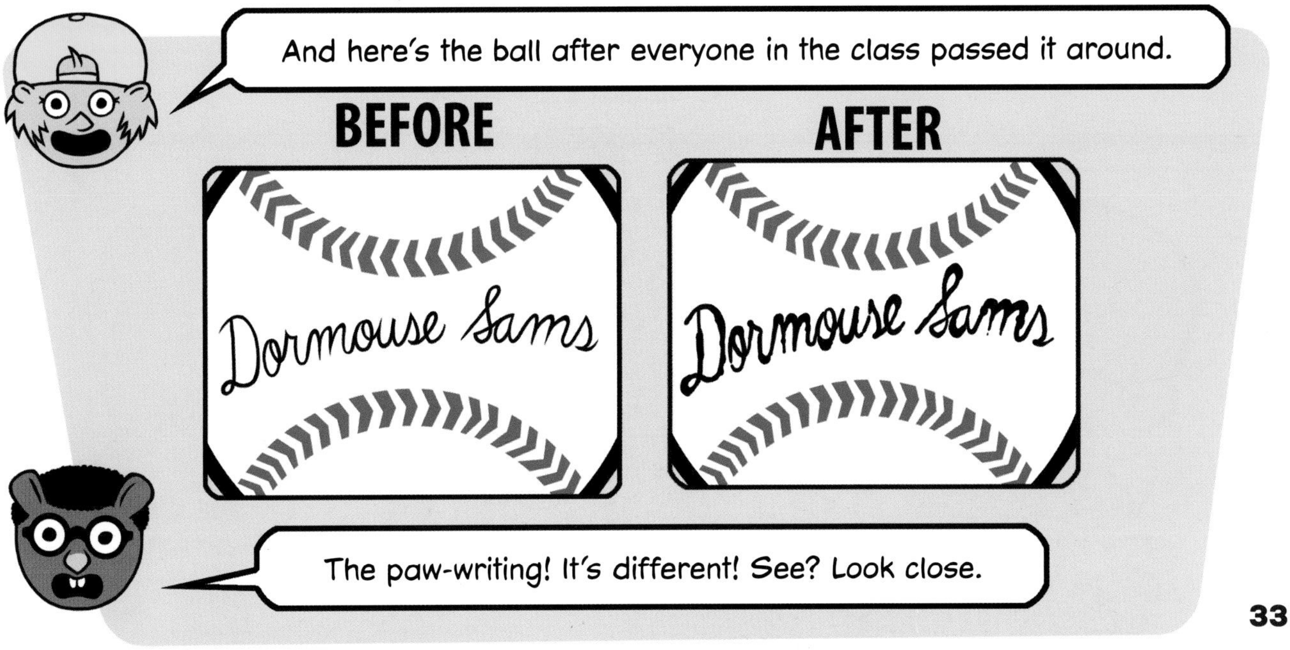
And here's the ball after everyone in the class passed it around.
BEFORE
Dormouse Sams
AFTER
Dormouse Sams
The paw-writing! It's different! See? Look close.

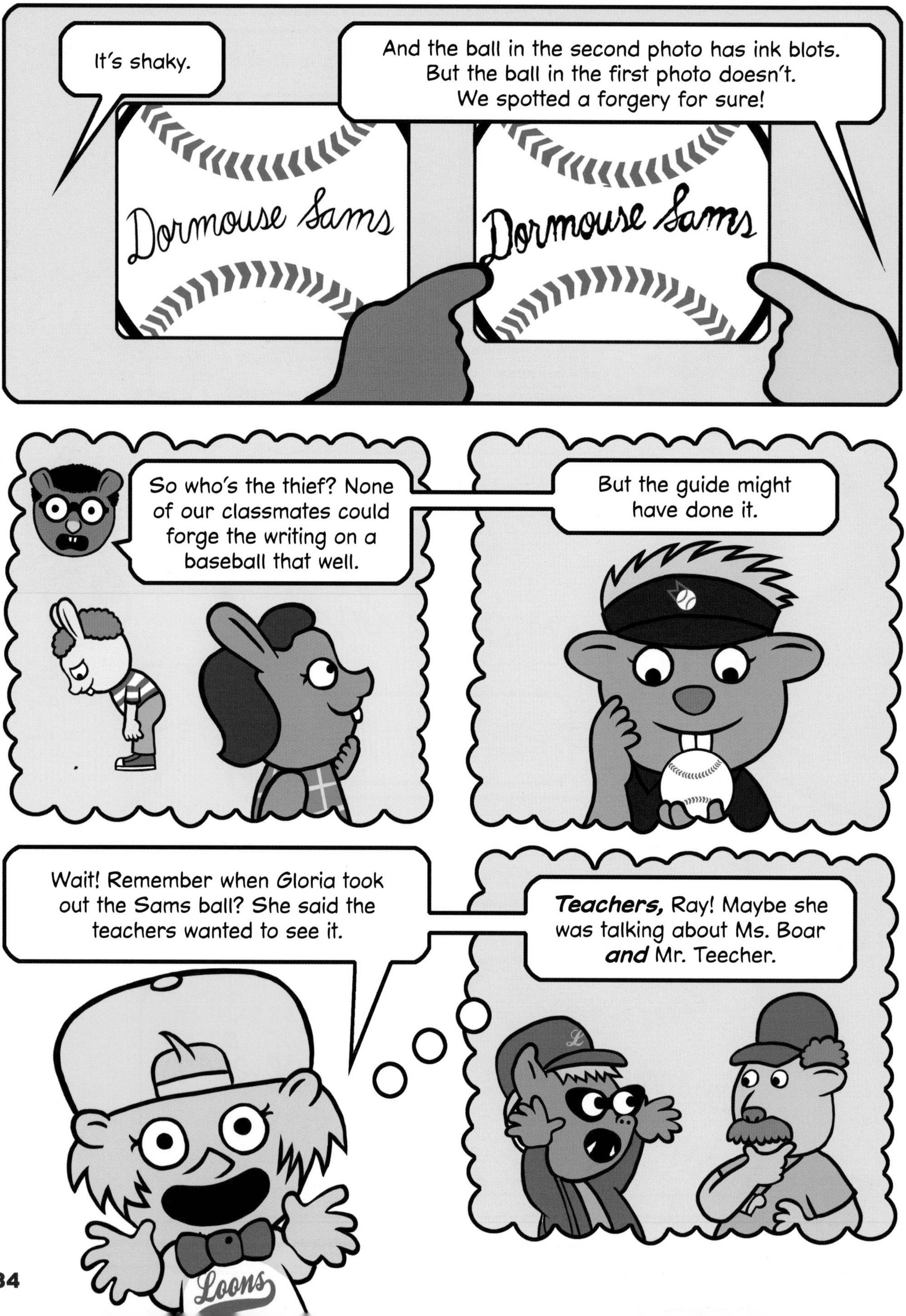
It's shaky.
And the ball in the second photo has ink blots. But the ball in the first photo doesn't. We spotted a forgery for sure!
Dormouse Sams
Dormouse Sams
So who's the thief? None of our classmates could forge the writing on a baseball that well.
But the guide might have done it.
Wait! Remember when Gloria took out the Sams ball? She said the teachers wanted to see it.
Teachers, Ray! Maybe she was talking about Ms. Boar *and* Mr. Teecher.
Loons

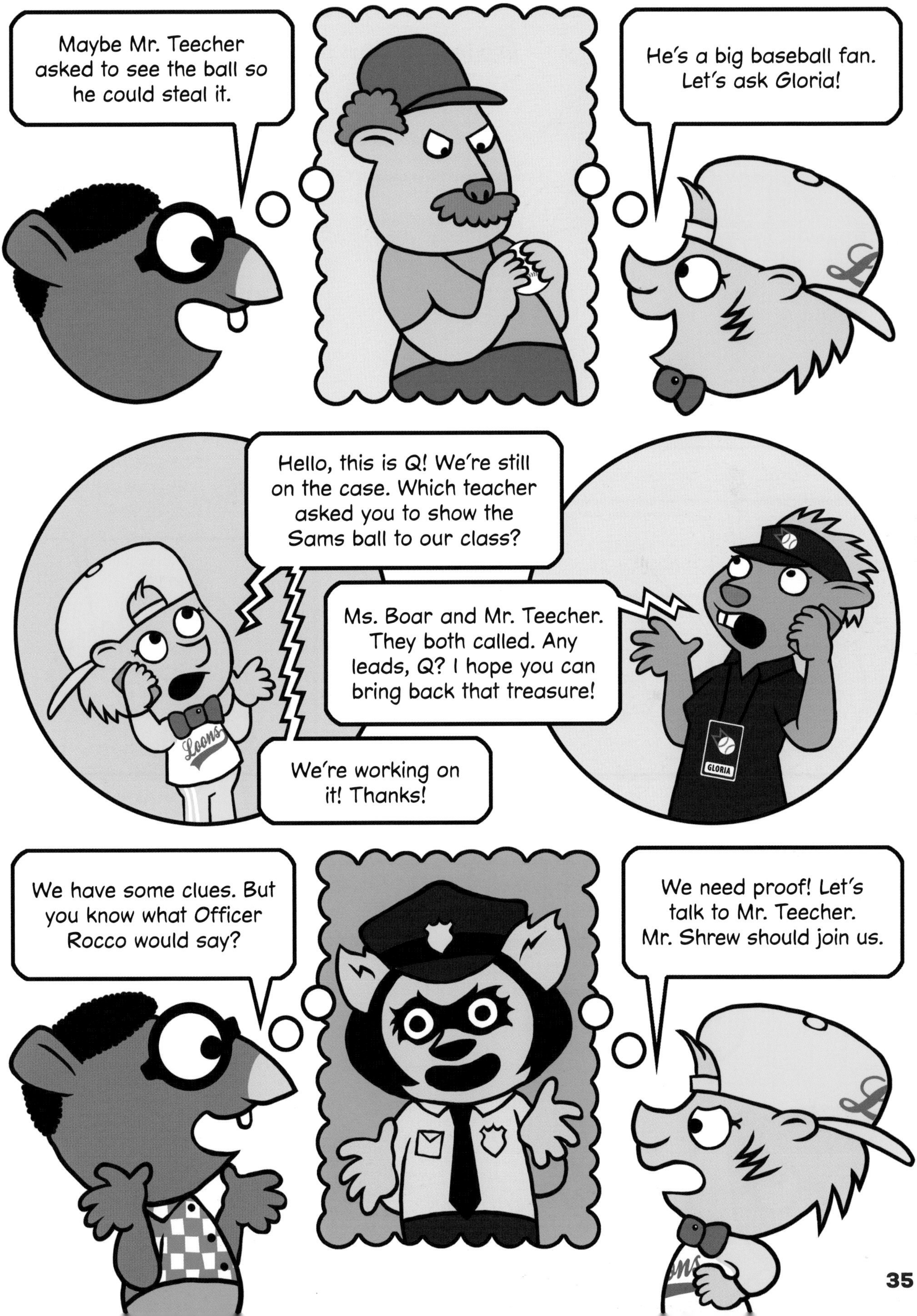
Maybe Mr. Teecher asked to see the ball so he could steal it.
He's a big baseball fan. Let's ask Gloria!
Hello, this is Q! We're still on the case. Which teacher asked you to show the Sams ball to our class?
Ms. Boar and Mr. Teecher. They both called. Any leads, Q? I hope you can bring back that treasure!
We're working on it! Thanks!
Loons
GLORIA
We have some clues. But you know what Officer Rocco would say?
We need proof! Let's talk to Mr. Teecher. Mr. Shrew should join us.

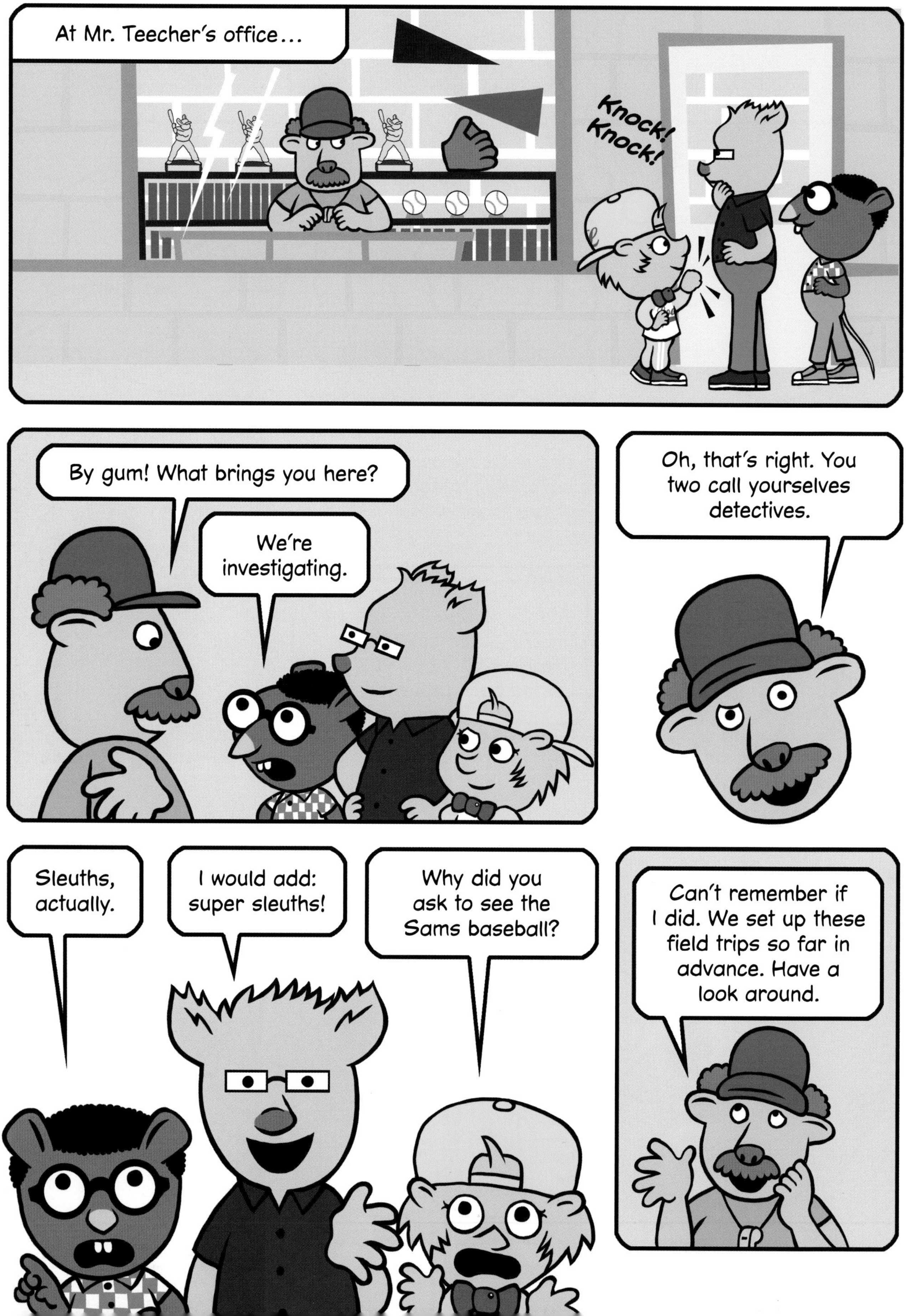
At Mr. Teecher's office...
Knock! Knock!
By gum! What brings you here?
We're investigating.
Oh, that's right. You two call yourselves detectives.
Sleuths, actually.
I would add: super sleuths!
Why did you ask to see the Sams baseball?
Can't remember if I did. We set up these field trips so far in advance. Have a look around.

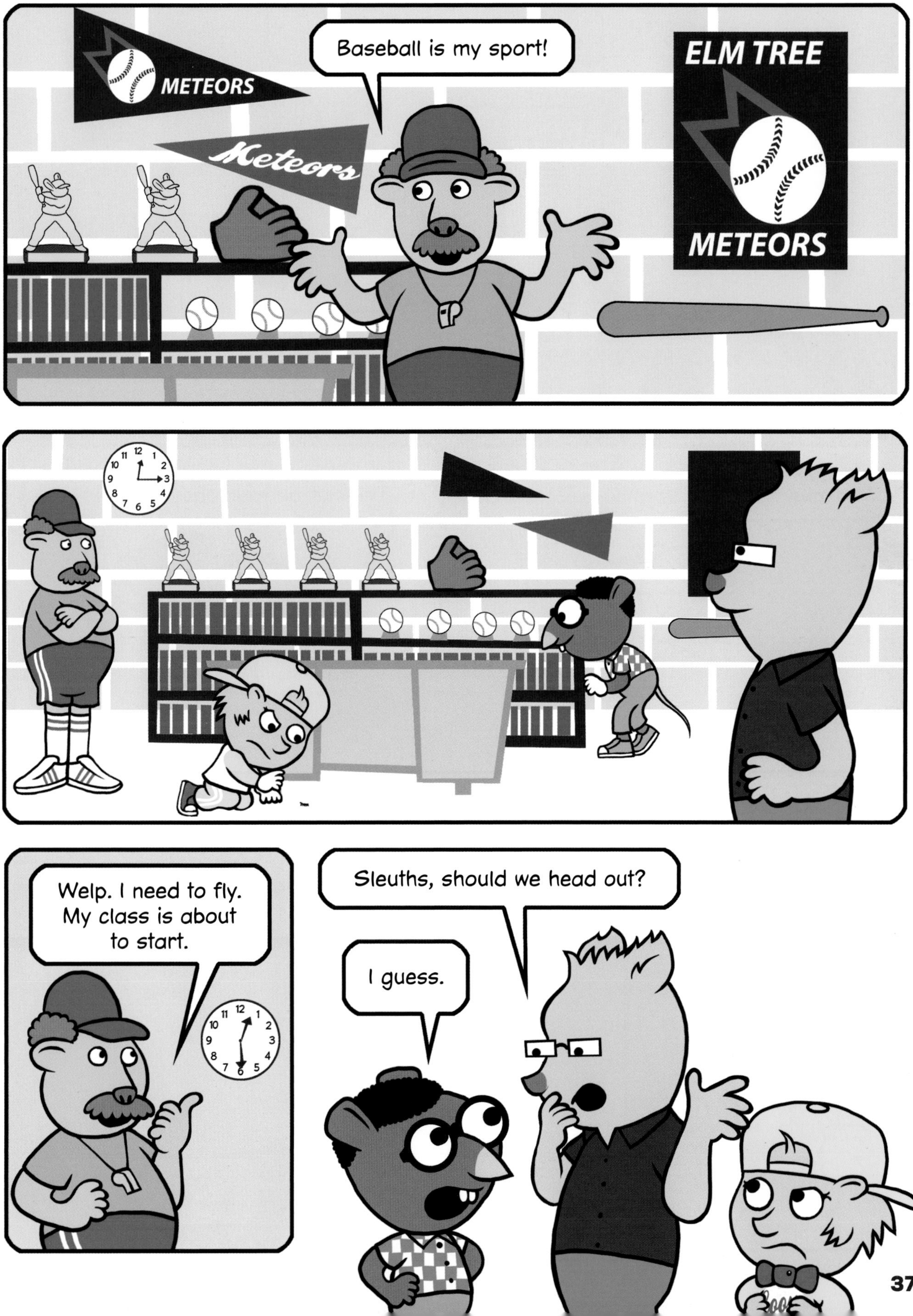
METEORS
Meteors
Baseball is my sport!
ELM TREE
METEORS
Welp. I need to fly. My class is about to start.
Sleuths, should we head out?
I guess.

CHAPTER EIGHT
Evidence

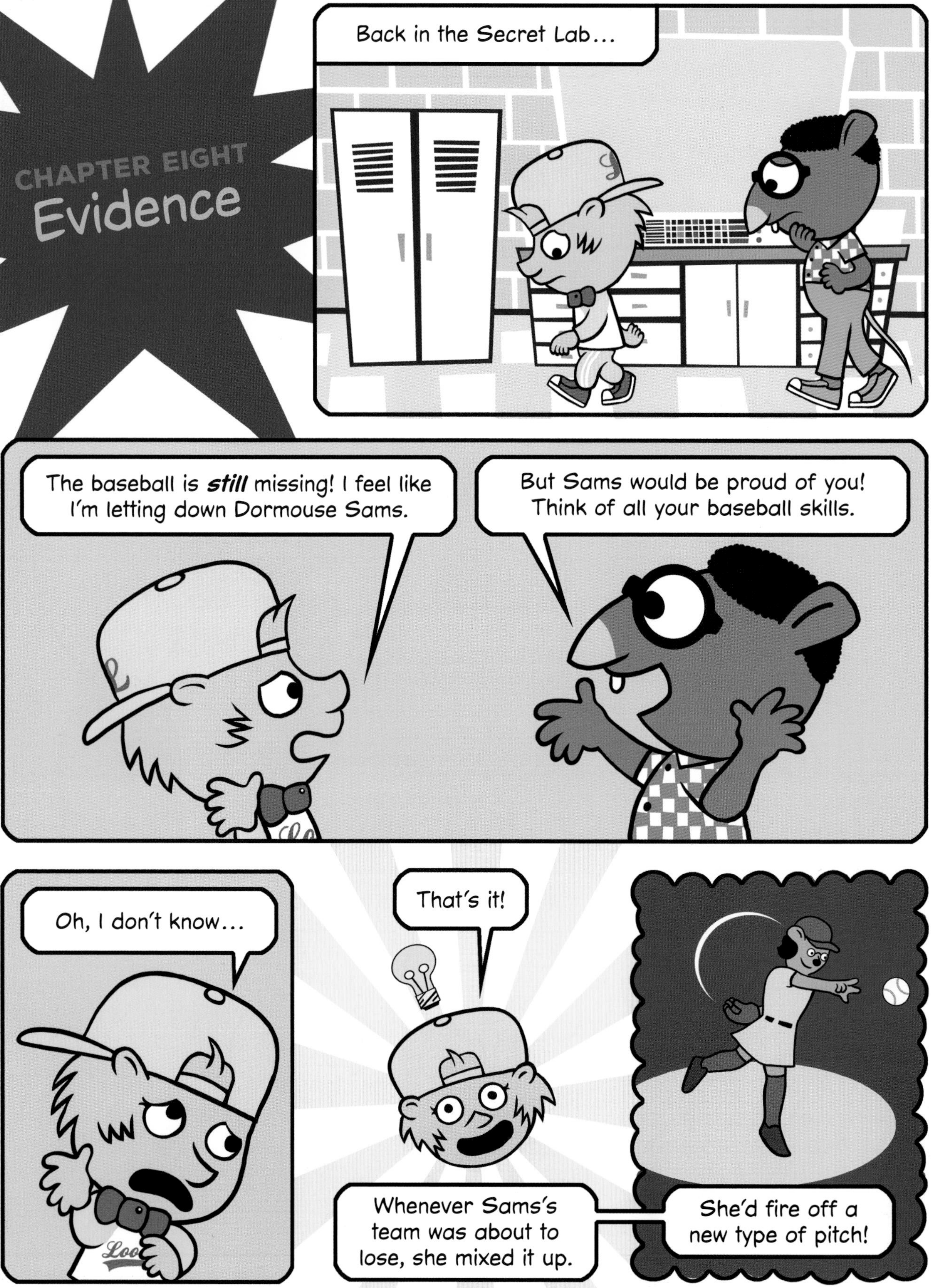

Back in the Secret Lab...
The baseball is ***still*** missing! I feel like I'm letting down Dormouse Sams.
But Sams would be proud of you! Think of all your baseball skills.
Oh, I don't know...
That's it!
Whenever Sams's team was about to lose, she mixed it up.
She'd fire off a new type of pitch!

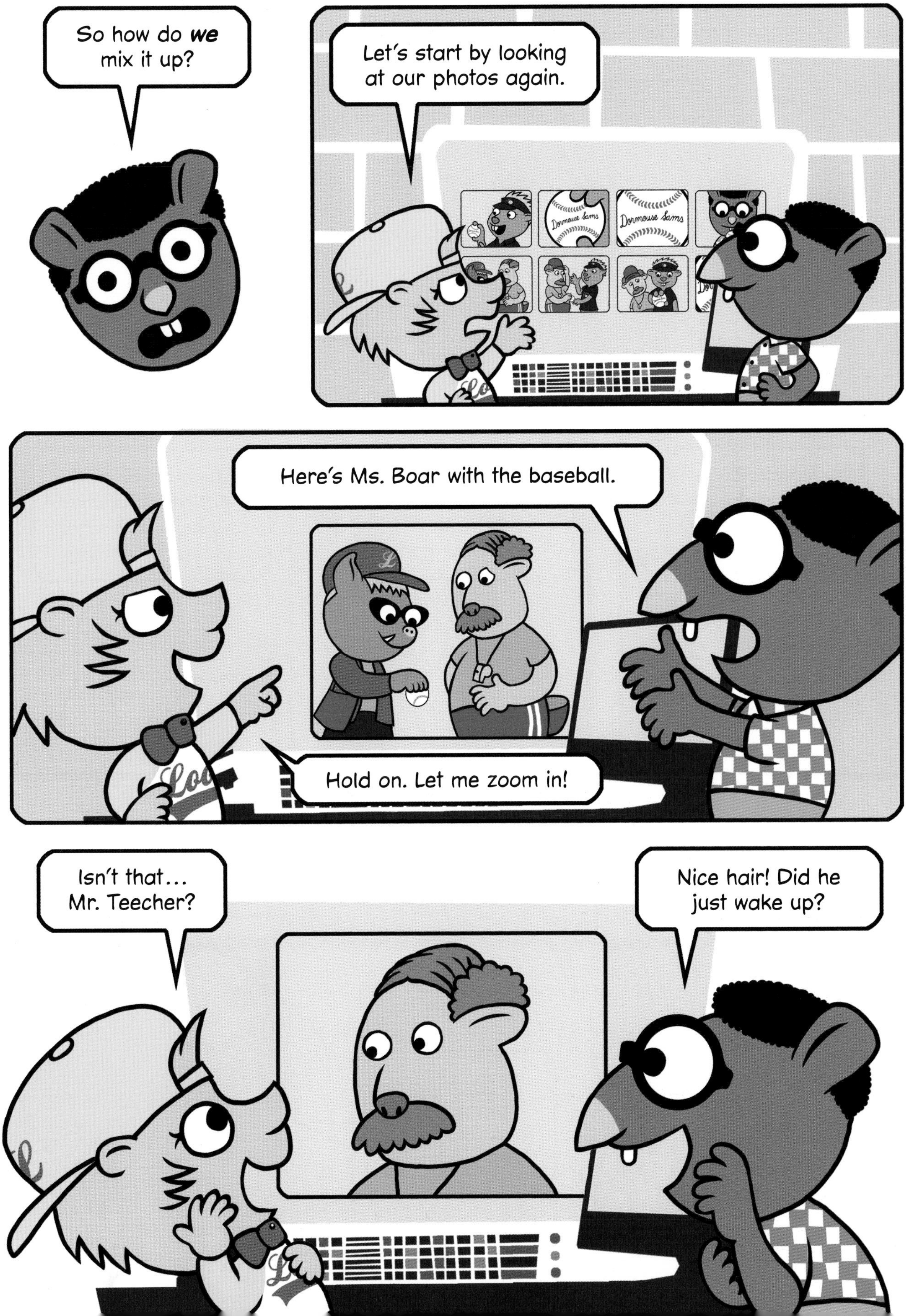
So how do **we** mix it up?
Let's start by looking at our photos again.
Dormouse Sams
Here's Ms. Boar with the baseball.
Hold on. Let me zoom in!
Isn't that… Mr. Teecher?
Nice hair! Did he just wake up?

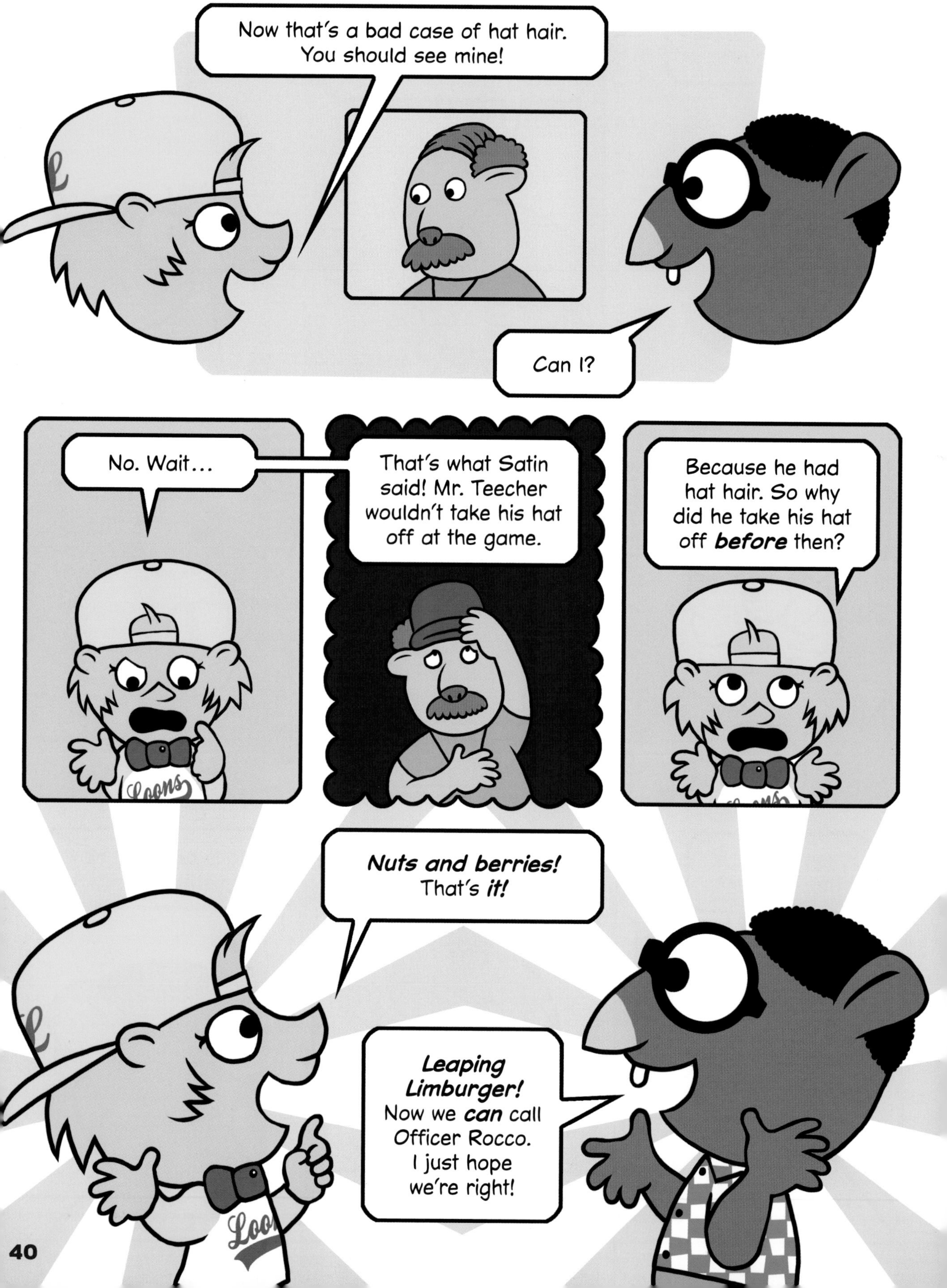

Now that's a bad case of hat hair. You should see mine!
Can I?
No. Wait...
That's what Satin said! Mr. Teecher wouldn't take his hat off at the game.
Because he had hat hair. So why did he take his hat off *before* then?
Nuts and berries! That's *it!*
Leaping Limburger! Now we *can* call Officer Rocco. I just hope we're right!

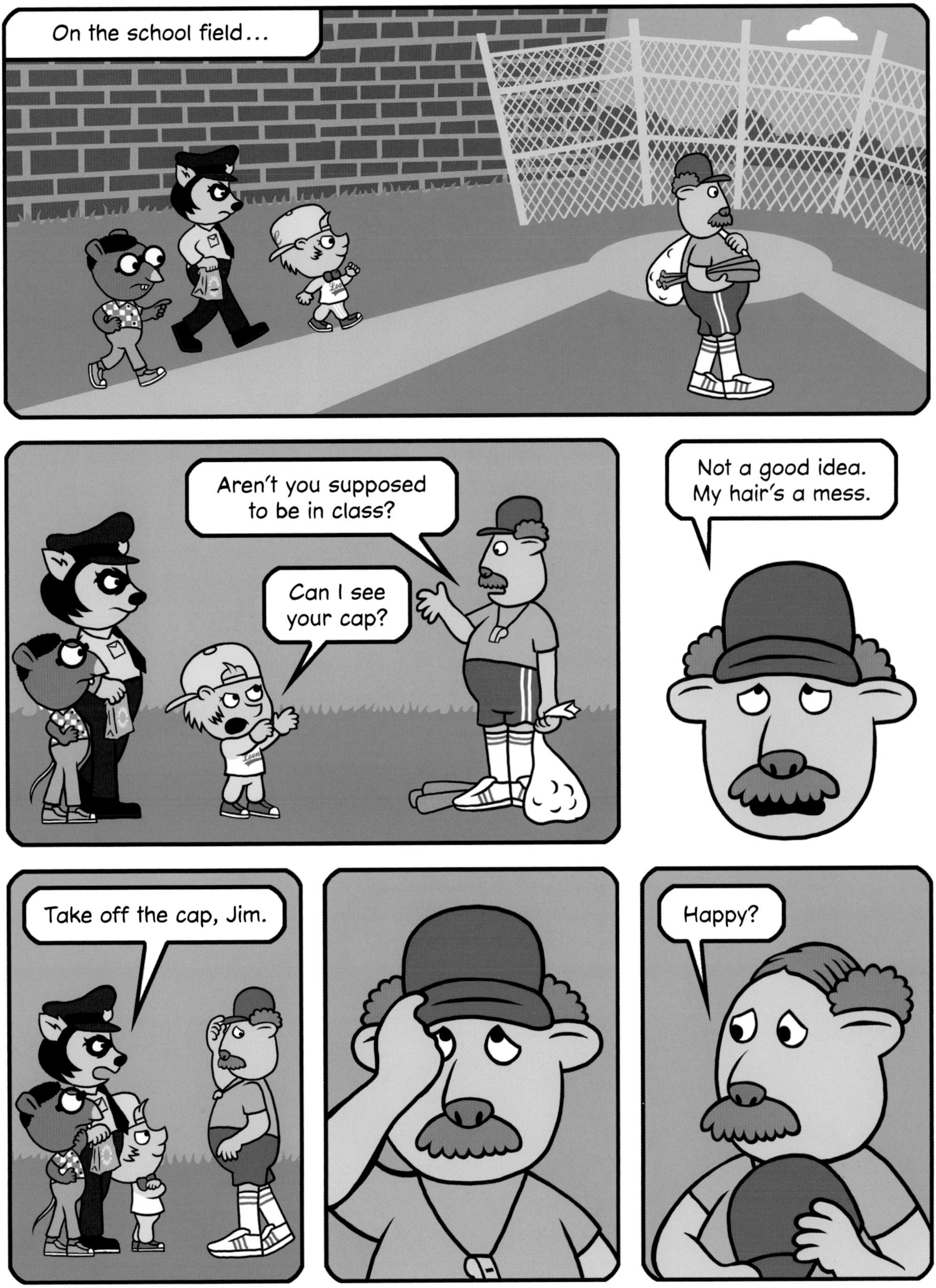
On the school field...
Aren't you supposed to be in class?
Can I see your cap?
Not a good idea. My hair's a mess.
Take off the cap, Jim.
Happy?

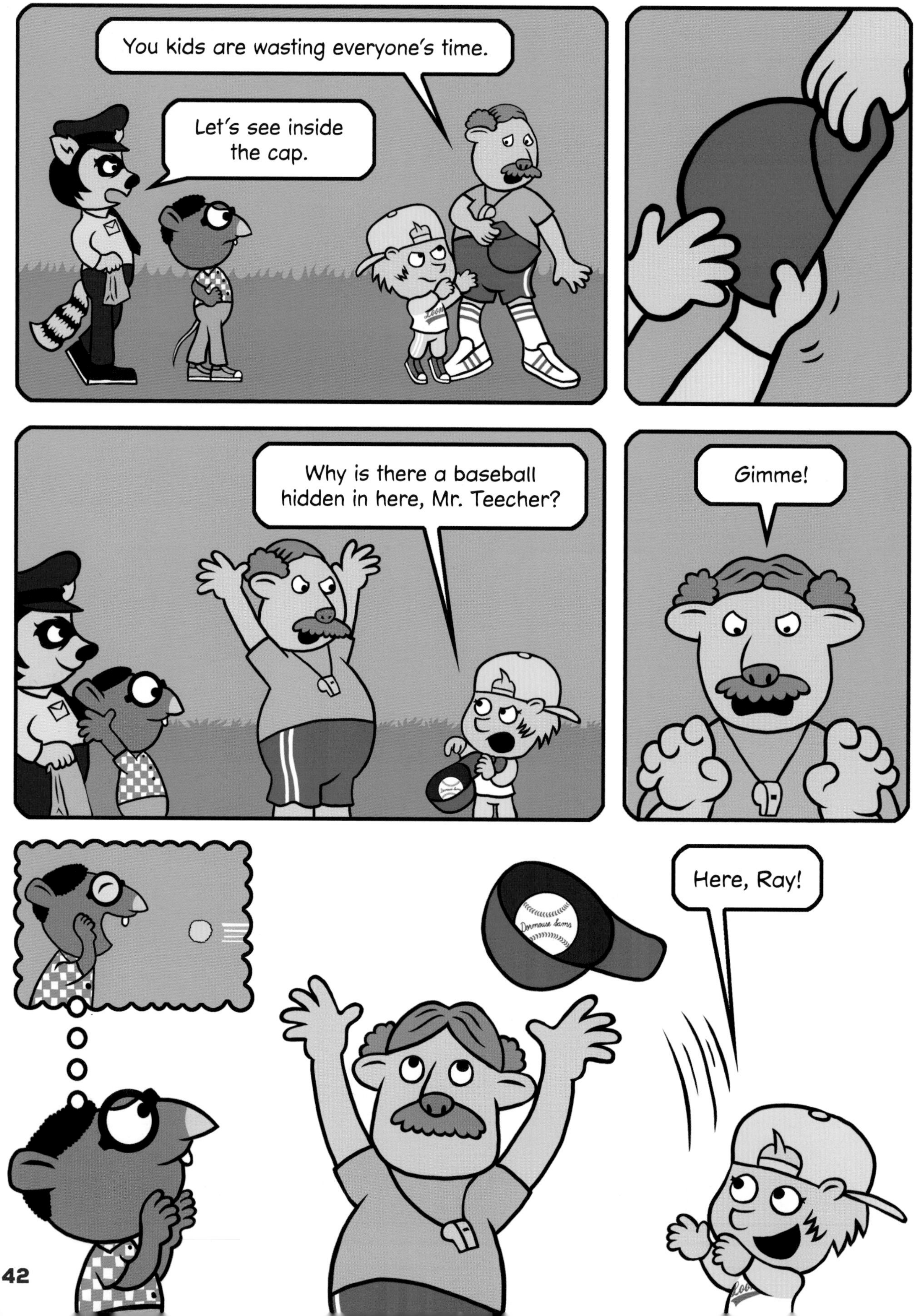
You kids are wasting everyone's time.
Let's see inside the cap.
Why is there a baseball hidden in here, Mr. Teecher?
Gimme!
Here, Ray!

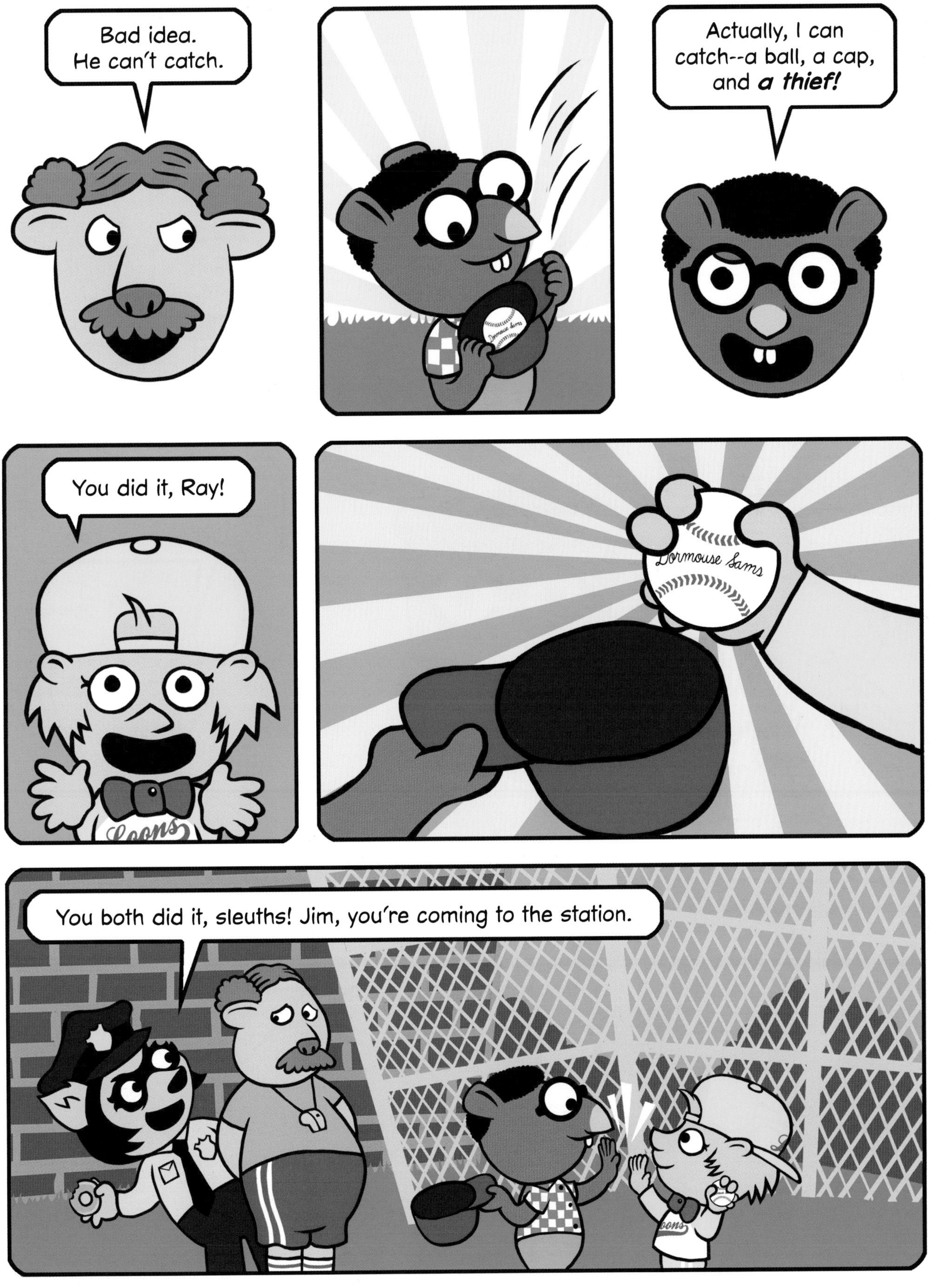
Bad idea.
He can't catch.
Dormouse Sams
Actually, I can catch--a ball, a cap, and ***a thief!***
You did it, Ray!
Loons
Dormouse Sams
You both did it, sleuths! Jim, you're coming to the station.

CHAPTER NINE
Play Ball!

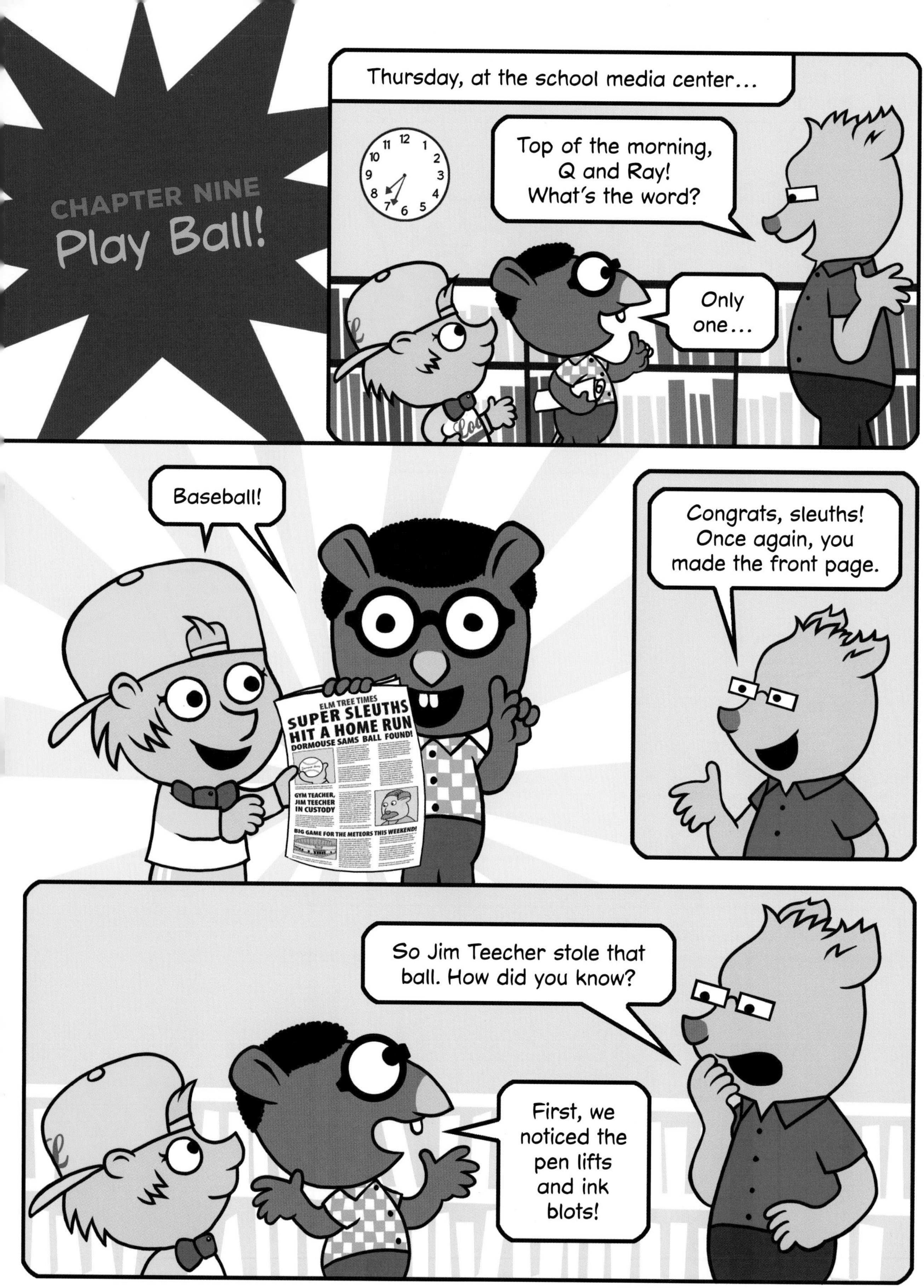

Thursday, at the school media center…
Top of the morning, Q and Ray! What's the word?
Only one…
Baseball!
ELM TREE TIMES
SUPER SLEUTHS HIT A HOME RUN
DORMOUSE SAMS BALL FOUND!
GYM TEACHER, JIM TEECHER IN CUSTODY
BIG GAME FOR THE METEORS THIS WEEKEND!
Congrats, sleuths! Once again, you made the front page.
So Jim Teecher stole that ball. How did you know?
First, we noticed the pen lifts and ink blots!

When Mr. Teecher tried to forge the writing on the newer ball, he lifted the pen. It made blots. Plus his fake writing was shaky.

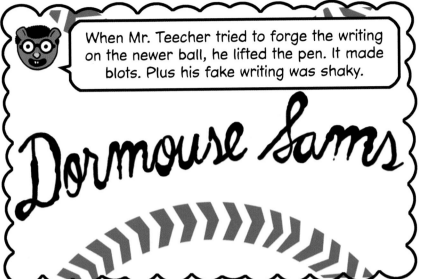

Dormouse Sams

During the tour, Mr. Teecher removed his hat.

But after the baseball went missing, he **wouldn't** remove it.

The ball had to be in his hat!

But why did Jim do it?

The money. He wasn't even a fan of Sams!

Because of him, we missed the opening pitch. And on Opening Day!

You're going to have a second chance! They want you to throw the opening pitch at the next Meteors game.

Nuts and berries!

And Ray, would you like to introduce Q to the fans?

You mean, on the microphone?

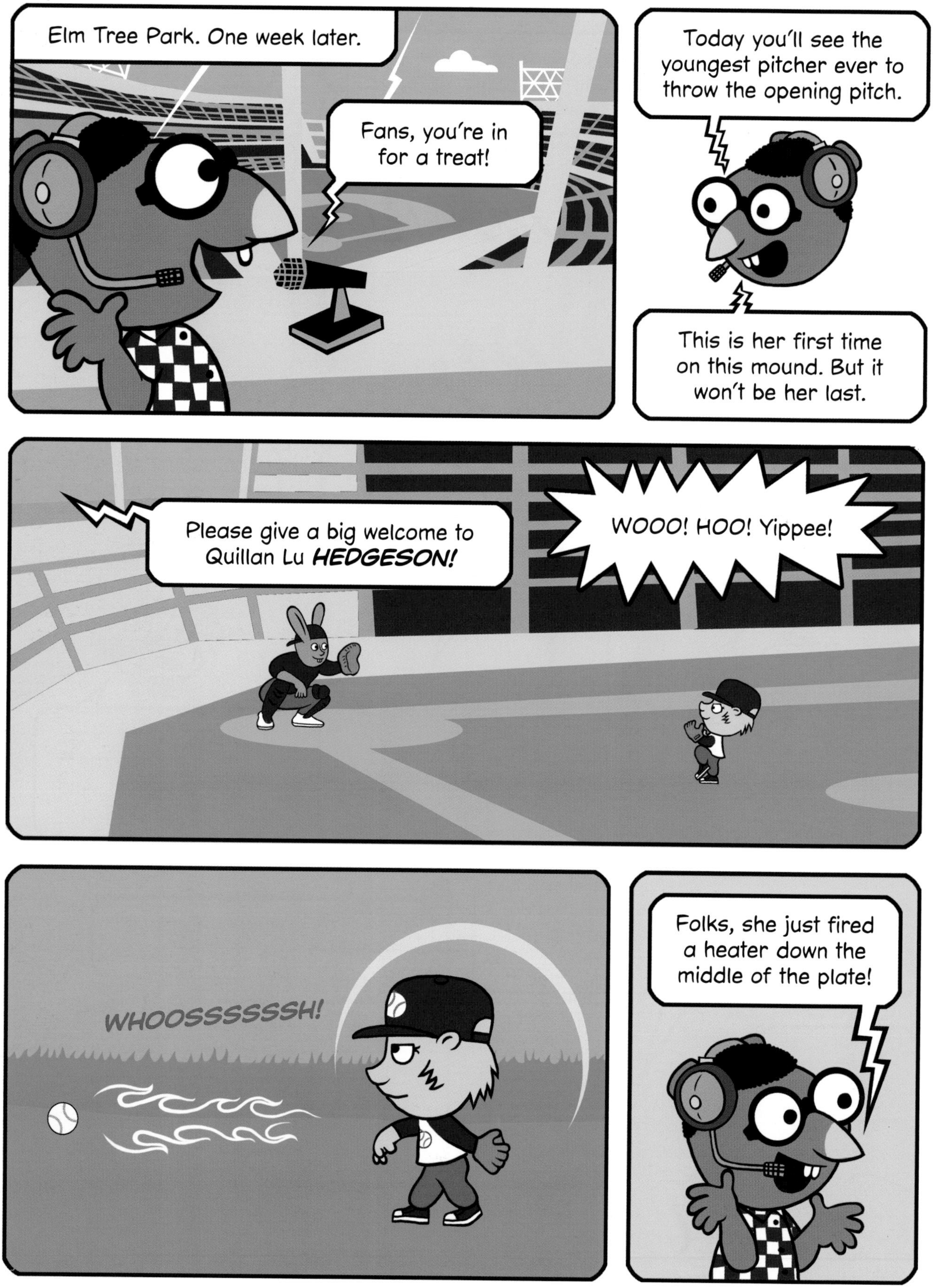
Elm Tree Park. One week later.
Fans, you're in for a treat!
Today you'll see the youngest pitcher ever to throw the opening pitch.
This is her first time on this mound. But it won't be her last.
Please give a big welcome to Quillan Lu HEDGESON!
WOOO! HOO! Yippee!
WHOOSSSSSSSH!
Folks, she just fired a heater down the middle of the plate!

Ten minutes later...

There's our ace!

Wowza! Just *wowza!*

Aren't you going to tell Ray to settle down, Ms. Boar?

Not today! I'm very proud of you, Q! You too, Ray!

Besides, this isn't a school day. *Go Meteors!*

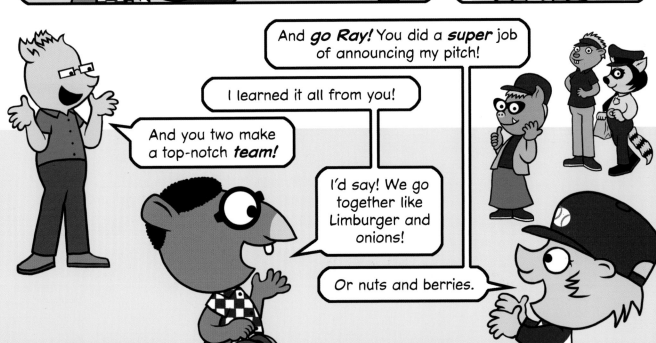

And *go Ray!* You did a *super* job of announcing my pitch!

I learned it all from you!

And you two make a top-notch *team!*

I'd say! We go together like Limburger and onions!

Or nuts and berries.

ABOUT THE AUTHOR

Trisha Speed Shaskan has written more than forty books for children, including the Q & Ray series and *Punk Skunks*, both of which are illustrated by her husband, Stephen Shaskan. As a child, Trisha played baseball at the park and softball on a team. Trisha and Stephen live in Minneapolis, Minnesota, with their cat, Eartha, and dog, Bea. Visit her at trishaspeedshaskan.com.

ABOUT THE ILLUSTRATOR

Stephen Shaskan is the author and illustrator of the picture books *A Dog Is a Dog*, *Big Choo*, *Max Speed*, *Toad on the Road: A Cautionary Tale*, *Toad on the Road: Mama and Me*, and *The Three Triceratops Tuff*. He's also the illustrator of *Punks Skunks*. Stephen is super excited to be creating the Q & Ray graphic novel series, since he grew up collecting, reading, and drawing comic books. Visit him at stephenshaskan.com.

FUN FACTS

In 1942 many young men in the United States were drafted to serve in World War II. People involved with baseball began to worry about the sport. With the young men away at war, baseball teams were short on players. Baseball parks were in danger of closing. And so a group of businesspeople created the All-American Girls Professional Baseball League (AAGPBL). This league operated from 1943 to 1954. During that time, more than six hundred women played professional baseball.

One of the best players in the AAGPBL was Doris Sams. For seven years, Doris Sams played for the Lassies. This team was based in Muskegon, Michigan, and later Kalamazoo, Michigan. She was the only player to be named to the AAGPBL all-star team as both a pitcher and outfielder. During the 1952 season, Sams set a record by hitting twelve home runs. She inspired the character Dormouse Sams too!